Slowly He Drew Her Close

lowering his head, taking her mouth with his. She pushed at him for a moment but a sweet, tremulous melting was spreading through her, and she gave herself wholly into his arms, letting her hands stray up to caress the back of his neck.

He held the kiss, moved his mouth wooingly, insistently, over hers till she thought that she would fall if he didn't hold her. She had never felt like this before. It swept her off-balance, destroyed judgment, memory, everything but the closeness of him, the harsh tenderness of his lips and arms, and suddenly she hoped that this magic moment of love would never end. . . .

More Romance from SIGNET

A Special Kind of Love

by
Kristin Michaels

A SIGNET BOOK
NEW AMERICAN LIBRARY
TIMES MIRROR

SIGNET TRADEMARK REG. U.S. PAT. OFF. AND FOREIGN COUNTRIES
REGISTERED TRADEMARK—MARCA REGISTRADA
HECHO EN CHICAGO, U.S.A.

SIGNET, SIGNET CLASSICS, MENTOR, PLUME AND MERIDIAN BOOKS
are published by The New American Library, Inc.,
1301 Avenue of the Americas, New York, New York 10019

First Signet Printing, June, 1976

1 2 3 4 5 6 7 8 9

PRINTED IN THE UNITED STATES OF AMERICA

For Pi Farr,
dear friend

A Special
Kind of Love

1

The road Aunt Corinth Redwine had marked turning off the freeway north of Houston was for a time a normal, civilized, well-behaved if rather narrow two-lane road. Then it became dirt, and the next fork was incredible. "Oil Company Road" Aunt Corinth had labeled it, and Randy noticed pumping jacks working away off to the side.

Mud puddles resembling lakes and water crept over the edge of the road from swampy grasslands. Even after a flight from New York, Randy had hardly noticed the hour on the freeway, but steering through this section of East Texas known as the Big Thicket was making her taut in the arms and shoulders. And Aunt Corinth's scribbled notes condemned her to ten miles of this atrocity.

Suddenly she was surrounded by giant trees, vines, flowers of every color. Against the leafy canopy, she glimpsed a flash of wings—a huge woodpecker with a red kingfisher-like crest, white surrounding the black center of his underwings. How big he was! She held her breath in wonder, but he was gone in a flash.

She stopped at a bridge, or rather, the bridge stopped her. It was lengths of pipe contained by a frame. No sides. I can't, she thought. What if the pipes rolled apart? Or if she veered a little and fell off into that wretched water? Still, what was she to do? She hadn't seen a house since she left the paved road at the town of Muscateen an hour ago. And since no pile of wrecks heaped the river below, whatever vehicles had dared the peculiar structure must have made it.

Commending herself to whatever power aided people who came to stay with disabled older relatives, Randy gritted her teeth and started across. The pipes seemed to shift. They certainly groaned, louder even than the prayerful sounds Randy was making.

Then the pipes seemed to sway. Randy eased the car along as gently as she could, but when the front wheels touched earth she accelerated quickly in a heartfelt urge to be off that horrifying bridge.

That was a mistake. The tires skidded to one side and even though she followed the direction of the skid while trying for control, the car's front was mired into a black morass.

She tried reversing, turning the steering wheel till her arms ached, but the car only growled, wheezed, coughed, and snorted. It didn't move except to sink in more snugly, as if it were tired of the journey and glad to rest.

Randy gnawed her lip and glanced frantically around—she saw only thick green wilderness. She'd have to look for help. Clambering in back, she was crawling out a window when a voice said, "So there you are!"

Randy stopped, half in and half out, then extricated herself with as much wobbly dignity as possible to confront a tall young man in khakis.

"How did you manage to do that?" he inquired, with an incredulous glance at the car before his gray eyes swept back to her. "I'll have to haul you out," he sighed resignedly. "Micajah'll help if I can find him. Right now we'd better get you along to Miss Corinth—you *are* her niece, I suppose?"

His tone suggested shock that her aunt could have such a feckless relative. "I—I'm not used to this kind of driving," she said, wishing she could get this patronizing backwoodsman on the turnpike at rush hour.

He nodded, and for the first time the ghost of a smile touched his long mouth. "Sort of guessed that. Never mind, it happens to natives."

He fairly lifted her across a wide puddle, then vaulted across to wedge flattish stones in front of the rear tires. "That should keep the situation from deteriorating further," he said. "Maybe we'd better take your luggage in case you need something from it before I get your car out."

Freeing her keys from the ignition, he opened the trunk and swung out her foldover hangup bag and pullman. Hampered by these, he walked around the puddle rather than leaping it, which gave Randy a chance to see him.

Thick reddish-brown hair that looked as if it had been hacked off curled about an angular face weathered to a shade that made his clear gray eyes a startling contrast. He wore heavy laced boots, and his khakis were faded and stained. He must be a lumberjack or oil worker, Randy thought. He was certainly different from Greg or anyone else she'd met.

Randy was glad she wore sandals that let her reach the

2

forest-green pick-up before he did so that she could scramble into the cab while he stowed her luggage in the back.

"I'm sorry to cause all this trouble," she said when he climbed up front and put the truck in gear. "If there's a garage—"

"No problem," he shrugged, slowing down for the worst mudholes, which had increased as if the ground was lower and more prone to overflow from the boggy surroundings. "But that car won't be much use to you here. When we get it out, why not let Micajah and me drop it off back at Muscateen?"

"Oh, I couldn't do that! Such a lot of bother—"

"Garbage! My dear young lady, people have to depend on each other out here, and we all owe Miss Corinth. Just give me your rental contract and you can pay me later." Closing off that subject, he spared her a surprisingly nice smile. "You have to be Miranda Redwine. I'm Travis Lee, one of your aunt's admirers. Do you remember her at all?"

"Not too well." Randy's father had been reared from the age of ten by his older sister. She had economized stringently in order to send him to Rice University in Houston. He had gone on to graduate school at Columbia where he met and married Randy's mother, and where they had both taught history. They had shared so much that it seemed inevitable that they shared death two years ago when their car skidded on ice. They had been buried at Randy's mother's home near Williamsburg.

Aunt Corinth had sent a rather incoherent telegram about not being able to come because of a cormorant and several loons and boobies, but Randy had been too stricken at the time to try to decipher that message.

"Aunt Corinth used to visit us at Christmas," she told Travis as they jounced along. "But about ten years ago she stopped coming. She'd accumulated a lot of pets and said it was hard to get anyone to take care of them properly while she was away."

"That could be a problem," Travis conceded gravely. "You're her only close kin?"

"She had a sister named Ephesus who died in San Francisco a few years ago, and the oldest brother, Sidon, was a missionary in the Amazon who disappeared long ago."

Travis shook his head. "Seems a shame for a family with such names to hover on the verge of extinction. I trust, Miranda, that you'll see that the Redwine vintage isn't lost.

3

Though I suppose," he added, between a smile and a sigh, "that it's too much to hope for another Corinth. If you haven't been in close touch, it's rather noble of you to undertake your present chore."

"I always liked her," Randy said. "She never talked down and would take me to do things my parents didn't have time for. Anyhow, she's the nearest to a grandmother I've got."

"You're lucky to be having such a long vacation," Travis remarked. "Your boss must be pretty lenient."

Lenient? Greg Hathaway?

Randy had worked for almost two years without taking time for vacation or illness, two long years in which Summit Advertising, under Greg's driving, brash leadership, had taken several hefty accounts away from under the noses of long-established firms.

One of these accounts was Quality Lumber. Quality wanted to upgrade its environmental appeal, and the fact that the company owned land near Aunt Corinth was probably what had edged Greg into agreeing to Randy's four-week absence.

"You *have* worked valiantly," he conceded, pushing his black hair back from his forehead and pacing his office like a cramped panther. "You deserve the time, Randy, I'm not arguing that." He stopped and caught her wrists, pulling her against him. "But it's not just that I need you in Research! It's going to be a damned dull life without you for a month. Maybe three weeks—?"

"Stop blandishing!" she warned. "And unhand me, boss! Haven't we agreed such demonstrations are poor office procedure?"

"There's no one around but Tom and Sue. They know I love you."

And Sue Ferris, the pretty secretary with hair as freshly yellow as a baby chick's, was in love with Greg. Randy was sure of that, and she wished she were equally clear about her own feelings for Greg. He was exciting, and it was fun to be taken one time to Trader Vic's and the next date to some bistro. Last year they had almost drifted into an engagement.

Lately, Greg had been asking her to set a date. His growing insistence on marriage was one more reason why she welcomed a chance to get away for a sizable chunk of time.

She wanted to rest up from his charming, sweeping impatience, to try to think clearly. And she couldn't help but feel that Sue was entitled to a few weeks without competition.

4

Randy suspected that in love as in business, Greg had a single-track mind. He would keep at an objective till he achieved it because that was the way he'd managed to head his own agency by the time he was thirty. She also knew that once a goal was definitely proved unobtainable, Greg dropped it and, without a second's regret, concentrated on a new aim.

When Randy had made it known that she was taking her long-delayed vacation in the Big Thicket of Texas, Greg stopped his plaintive remarks and studied her appraisingly.

"All right," he said. "Go! But see what you can find to power the Quality account—show how they're doing good things down there—"

"What if they're not?" Randy vaguely remembered fulminations against lumber companies from one of Aunt Corinth's infrequent letters.

Greg frowned. "They pay salaries and that's good," he said. "You'll dig up something." Heedless of her protest, Tom's amused look, and Sue's envious one, he kissed her firmly and led her to the door. "I want you back here in exactly four weeks," he decreed. "If you're not, I'll come after you, and the fact that we had to honeymoon in East Texas will always be your fault!"

Because of all this and her own confused feelings about Greg, Randy made a wry face before she responded to Travis Lee's comment.

"My boss isn't so lenient, but he knows I worked far beyond the call of duty when he was starting the agency. Of course I just said I was going. Otherwise I'd be delving into ways Quality Lumber looks like nature's fairy godmother."

"Quality Lumber? You work for them?"

"It's one of our big new accounts. I'm with an advertising outfit."

Travis snorted. "And you'd make Attila the Hun look good if he paid you?"

That was an aspect of the business that sometimes troubled Randy, but she'd soothed her conscience thus far by declining to work on promotion for clients she believed to be hustling the public. She had taken the job temporarily while hunting for a place to use her journalism degree, and far back in her mind lurked the feeling that she hadn't yet found what she really wanted to do.

"Do you know anything about Quality's operation here?" she asked.

Travis took a deep profane breath. "Lady, I can *show* you

5

their product. Thousands of acres of slash pine growing where Quality bulldozed out oaks, beech, hickory, magnolia, hundreds of varieties of plants and flowers. Where you get only pine, you get pine borer beetle infestations, which are treated by spraying insecticide from planes. And insecticides do nasty things to birds, fish—and, eventually, people. Even if Quality had a right to treat the land that way, there's no way of containing such damage within property limits."

Travis paused, obviously throttling back a good deal more. "I want you to do one thing before you go back to New York and start glamorizing Quality. Take a half day to let me show you what they're doing."

He had to be exaggerating. Thrusting out her chin, Randy said, "They must have fired you. Or you're in a competing business."

"Damn right I am," he said with a harsh laugh. "I try to salvage some of what Quality destroys, and when I get disgusted enough to feel like getting out of the Thicket, there's Miss Corinth to remind me that quitters never won a fight." He shot Randy a dark glance. "Wait till she hears you're supposed to do a selling job on Quality!"

Randy sat stiffly erect. "I should hope that since I've come to help her, my aunt won't be as rude as you are. How can you bear to have me contaminating your truck?"

Insultingly, he scanned her ears and neck, gaving a tolerant shrug. "You look clean enough. Anyhow, I've toted alligators for Miss Corinth."

Alligators!

Speechless, Randy simmered for a few minutes till she remembered a question that had been nagging her ever since her aunt's rather garbled phone call. "How did Aunt Corinth break her leg? I've asked several times but she didn't seem to hear too well."

Travis Lee chuckled. "She's got selective hearing, Miss Corinth does. She was brushing her teeth when Penzance nipped her. She jumped and fell against the tub, and then she slipped on the tiles. She was lucky, at her age, to only break a leg. She's pretty touchy about the way it happened. Maybe you shouldn't mention it."

"Penzance is her dog?"

"No. He's a cormorant."

"A cormorant?" Randy echoed.

Travis cocked a puzzled eyebrow, scanned Randy's face,

then broke into startled laughter. "You don't know!" he gasped. "You really don't know."

"Know what?" Randy demanded. Was the man crazy?

"You'll see," he told her.

He pulled the truck sharply in a half-circle and stopped in front of a long, low vine-covered house that seemed to have grown right out of the forest.

2

A jumble of hounds rose up and started belling, their long ears of various colors hanging almost to the ground, tails wagging violently as they swarmed about the truck.

"Down!" Travis commanded, wading through the dogs as he loped around to help Randy out.

A wiry small man appeared in the doorway and gave a whistle that brought immediate calm. "Hush up, you loud-mouth hooligans!" he scolded the hounds, who flocked around him. "You'll give that dratted cormorant the heaves and there'll be merry hell to pay!"

He strode toward Randy, looked at her with keen hazel eyes the shade of a turning oak leaf, and nodded. "Well, well, well! Pretty as a speckled pup with its eyes just opened! I'm Micajah Chance, Miss Randy. Come right in. Your aunt's been fidgetin' this last hour like a hen whose eggs won't hatch! Want I should give you a hand with those bags, Travis?"

"Want you should ride over to the bridge with me and help get Miss Redwine's car out of the mud," said Travis, easily handling the luggage while Micajah sprinted to open the screen door. "You can follow along to Muscateen so I can drop the car at the rental place."

Randy scarcely heard. The moment she stepped inside, it was like a remembered dream. A huge fireplace ruled the middle of the end of the room, and a quilting frame stood by it, brightly appliquéd blocks set in snowy cotton. A rosewood dulcimer lay on a bench and braided rag rugs softened mellow plank floors.

In an easy chair by the window sat Corinth Redwine, her short wispy red hair flaming in the late sunlight. Her eyes were russet, fox-alert in a thin, weathered face. A cast protruded from beneath her flowing brown cotton robe, and her leg was resting on a footstool.

On the open shelves beside her were several small cages

and half a dozen mixing bowls spread with paper towels, each having a small light bulb clipped to the rim. Each bowl and cage was inhabited by more or less tiny birds. They were all cheeping, and the feathered elders in the cages were pecking at the bars.

Aunt Corinth held out her arms. "Kiss me, child," she instructed. "Then you can help feed these babies—have to stuff 'em every half-hour, you know—and then we can visit."

Something like an animated muff peered out from behind Aunt Corinth's back. It made a chuckling sound and skidded past Randy to cavort around Travis till he put down Randy's luggage, picked up the beast, and tickled the long, dark brown creature's belly. It wriggled and giggled, stubby webbed feet flailing.

"Penelope's an otter," Aunt Corinth explained, in answer to Randy's half-frightened stare. "She adores men, Travis especially, the hussy!"

Gathering Randy to her, Aunt Corinth gave her head a pat, her cheek a kiss, and her linen pants suit a critical look. "Best change into something old, Miranda. This bird food is pretty messy. Travis, you'll show Miranda how to feed Penzance, won't you?"

"Sure, but he can wait till Micajah and I pull your niece's car out of the mud and turn it in at Muscateen." He gave Penelope a last tickle, set her down, and hefted the luggage.

"She get the preacher's room?"

"Yes. It may be a trifle musty but it should be clean. Hasn't been anything in it since you took Goldie off my hands, and I'm sure I hunted out all the mice fur and feathers."

"Please, Miss Corinth!" protested Travis. "Goldie isn't a proper name. She's Glory."

Aunt Corinth sniffed, reaching and mixing ingredients ranged on a table beside her. *"Gloria in excelsis Deo!"* she scoffed, measuring out vitamin drops. "What kind of label is that?"

Micajah noticed Randy's bemused expression and chuckled. "They're not fussin' about a gal," he explained. "Glory's a golden eagle who got her wing smashed by over fifty shotgun pellets." He shook his head. "Miracle that she lived, let alone ever flew again."

"All right," yielded the boyish-faced old woman. "I'm not the one to deny that a bird flying is like a singing prayer.

9

And when an eagle circles to the sun, it's an awesome lovely sight. But she'll always be Goldie to me."

"Glory," insisted Travis, and led the way through a big airy kitchen equipped with both fireplace and gas range, and a bedroom that must be Aunt Corinth's, which opened into a breezeway connecting to an addition that gave the house an L shape.

"What you've got here is the original 'shotgun' house with a couple of rooms added as the family grew and prospered," said Travis, opening the door to the newer section and thrusting through the luggage. "A 'shotgun' house was called that because you could stand in the front door and shoot straight back through the whole shebang. Folks started with a one-room cabin and built on as they could afford it."

Travis opened the door to the third room in the L section. He glanced from the high, dust-ruffled brass-knobbed bed covered with a breathtakingly handsome quilt to a triple-mirrored dresser, graceful writing desk, and rocking chair occupying a braided rug with a brass floor lamp in good reading position.

"I don't see mute nor feather of Glory." Travis put the pullman on a leather chest and undid the foldover, hanging it in a huge armoire gilded with leaves and grapes. "Better yet, Miss Corinth must have found all the bones and scraps." He paused in the door. "Your bathroom connects to the last room on the L." He seemed unable to repress a grin, which did good things to his strong, almost forbidding face. "Fortunately you don't have to share with Penzance!"

With that he departed, leaving the door open to the long screened porch. Since her aunt wanted her to help feed assorted birds, Randy made a quick change into comfortable old jeans and a shirt, paused in the kitchen for a drink of cool sweet water from the tap, and went back to the living room. The men were gone.

"Pull up a chair," said Corinth Redwine, dipping a swab stick without the cotton tip into the food mixture. "You can feed these older babies while I finish the young ones that still need a medicine dropper."

She tapped against one of the cages, made a kissing sound, and the little bird became all gaping mouth. "You need to put the food far back so it'll trigger the swallowing reflex," explained Aunt Corinth, depositing the food and giving the little creature two more bites while his tiny neighbors pecked away at their cages and bits of wood. She handed Randy the loaded swab stick.

"Go ahead, dear. The mite's hungry."

Flinching, Randy glanced helplessly from swab to gullet. How could such a minute creature have such a large beak and big mouth? "I—I'm afraid I'll hurt it," she stammered. "Puncture its throat or—or—"

"Fudge!" said Aunt Corinth impatiently. "Hurry, child. There are three more of those to feed, and if you don't move, you'll no sooner finish than you'll have to start over."

Thus admonished, Randy swallowed, set her teeth, and gingerly poked the swab stick down the cavernous throat. The moist food fell off quite handily as it touched inside. The bird swallowed and had its beak open greedily by the time Randy scooped up its next taste.

By the time she had given it half a dozen bites without dire results, Randy began to enjoy the experience. "How much do they eat?" she asked.

"Don't feed till they close up," her aunt warned. "Give Woody there another five or six bites and then get on to that little purple martin next to him. He's the only young one I have right now that isn't a woodpecker of some sort or other, but he can eat the same mixture." Aunt Corinth pressed gently on a medicine dropper as a tiny pin-feathered bird sucked at the thinner mixture Corinth held in a measuring cup.

"What's in the food?" Randy asked, much more sure of herself now as she fed the miniature martin. It was fun, once she stopped agonizing about impaling the recipient.

"Those bigger ones get ground beef mixed with turkey starter, vitamin drops, and water. The little ones don't get the meat."

Randy moved on to another woodpecker, who swallowed and then pecked eagerly at the stick. "Ruff's getting ready to start feeding himself," Aunt Corinth said. She handed over a jar lid. "Put some feed in this and let him take all he will, but you'll need to feed him some from the stick till he can manage completely alone."

"When do they get water?"

"You can get Ruff a lid full when you finish with the others. Tiny babies don't need more than they get in their food." Aunt Corinth laughed in a throaty expansive way that seemed strange coming from such a wisp of a person. "You ever see a mother bird fetch water to her brood?"

"I never saw one fetch anything," said Randy.

She fed the other young woodpeckers and got Ruff some water before she finished giving him his meal on the swab stick. "You say they have to be fed every half hour?" she asked.

"Not during the night," comforted her aunt. "Really young infants have to be fed every fifteen minutes, but fortunately these can all go longer. When it gets dark, we'll move them to my bedroom and they'll be fine till morning."

"How long have you been doing this?" Randy asked.

"Years. Always did try to help any wild hurt thing I came across, and now people bring me birds and animals. Travis helps a lot." She sighed and shifted the cast a little. "Of course a lot of the poor things are too far gone and die. Others are so crippled that they can't live in the wilds, and I keep them or find them homes. When the men get back, they can introduce you to the herons and egrets in the back yard who are too maimed to go free but who have a lot of fun anyway." She rubbed the cast on her leg, grimacing. "That dratted Penzance is almost well enough to join them, thank goodness! It'll be nice to have my bathroom to myself again."

Randy felt properly grateful that a nipping cormorant wasn't resident in her territory. And that she could sleep the night through without having to stuff hungry little mouths. "Shall I start something for dinner?" she asked.

"Micajah put a stew on the back burner, and Travis brought some bread and a pie his housekeeper baked. You might make tea while you're setting the table. Lay places for the men, child, they'll be starving."

Aunt Corinth leaned back, closing her eyes, and Randy, though completely astounded at having it blithely assumed that she would feed nestlings, cormorants, and heaven knew what else, felt a rush of compassion along with an uncontrollable need to laugh.

Her admirable if imperious relative opened one fox eye. "What's funny?"

"You, Aunt Corinth!" Randy choked. "I expected to plump your pillows and read to you, keep your mind off your leg, and fetch you tea and trays and posies!"

"Do you think I'd have called you down here for that?" Aunt Corinth's tawny head quivered with disgust at the thought. "Gracious, I can take care of myself. But the bird food has to be mixed fresh every other feed so the hamburger won't spoil, and there's just more than I can manage hobbling around. I couldn't have swung it this long without Travis, though he has his own work to tend to and just pops in and out."

"Micajah seems helpful."

Aunt Corinth hooted. "If I've told Micajah Chance once, I've told him a thousand times: I'll never marry a hunting man! Told him that since he was twenty and I sixteen. But his head's as hard as a cypress knee. *'Chances always been hunters,'*" she mimicked bitterly. "*'Got the same line of hounds and the same horn my great-grandpa brought from Virginia!'*"

Randy stared. "You mean you've cared about each other all this time and never married because he hunts?"

"That's exactly right." Aunt Corinth seemed a bit flushed, and her eyes took on a baleful gleam.

"B-but the hamburger for the birds—the fish for the birds!" protested Randy. "Don't you eat meat?"

"Well, yes," admitted Aunt Corinth slowly. "Ham and beef. Tame meat that's raised for the table."

"I'm not sure cows and pigs would see the difference," suggested Randy.

"There's a hell of a lot of difference," snapped her embattled aunt. "Wild creatures fend for themselves. It's as if they were—well, direct vassals of God without man in between. Anyhow," she concluded, "it comes down to how I feel, and that's *how* I feel, and I don't have to be reasonable for Micajah or anybody else."

It was refreshing to hear someone refuse to pay even lip service to logic. Randy grinned.

"All the same, I'm glad he's going to help feed the cormorant."

"Oh, he's a good man most ways," grudged Aunt Corinth. "Just stubborn. Set in his ways."

At that Randy burst out laughing. After a startled look, her aunt joined in. "How about that tea?" she demanded when their mirth had subsided to fitful splutters. "I'd favor sassafras myself. It's the big jar on the first shelf of the long cupboard. Mind you boil the bark about ten minutes."

"That I'll have to taste," decided Randy.

The moment she stepped in the kitchen, a flavorsome odor tantalized her. She put a small saucepan of water on the front burner, took the lid off a rich thick stew, and gave it a stir before locating the jar of red-brown sassafras bark.

Placing what seemed to be a sensible amount of tea in the

13

bubbling saucepan, she found some white stoneware plates and woven blue straw mats, and set the trestle table by the kitchen window. Ornately wrought sterling that must have been heirloom was jumbled in the drawer with cereal box-top stainless steel. Randy fished out enough silver for four and found a whole trove of snowy napkins in the bottom drawer. Then she got a crock of butter out of the refrigerator to soften.

The tea was a lovely amber rose color as she poured it into cups through a strainer.

"Sugar?" she called.

"Honey," smiled a voice from behind her at the screened back door. Whirling, she gazed into Travis Lee's deep gray eyes.

3

Her heart stopped, giving an awkward fumbling leap, then began to race absurdly. Stop it! she scolded herself. You're in love with Greg, aren't you? Almost engaged. And this skinny, scroungy, long-jawed backwoodsman doesn't approve of you one bit—even if he is almost smiling. He must smell the stew.

"Is there enough sassafras for Micajah and me?" he asked, ducking slightly to enter. "Pour out and I'll put in the honey. Want some in yours?"

While all too conscious of his nearness, she mutely strained two more cups of the spicily fragrant brew. He took the lid off an apothecary jar and stirred golden honey into each cup, then carried two of them into the other room. Randy followed with the remaining cups, handing one to Micajah since Travis had already served Aunt Corinth.

Micajah's hazel eyes twinkled as he thanked her. He must have come in through the front to have a private word with his scornful lady. He wore forest-green work clothes and moccasins, and his hair was so blond that it was silver or so silver that it was blond—a striking contrast to his leathery skin. He was as handsome in his way as Aunt Corinth in hers. Randy thought it a shame they had never married, and she smiled at him with special sweetness.

"Your car's turned in at Muscateen," he assured her. "Guess that means you'll just have to settle in and stay with us for good."

"I only got a month by blackmail and bribery," Randy laughed.

Travis regarded her somberly. "Should be natural talents for the job you're in."

"Why, you bigoted, self-righteous, judgment-passing churl!" began Randy.

"Judgment-passing?" mocked Travis, lifting one dark eyebrow in a way that made Randy ache to plant a toe in his lanky shin.

15

"Dirty pool, son," chided Micajah.

"I want to know what this is all about," cut in Aunt Corinth. "But it's time to feed the birds. Travis, will you help me while Micajah shows Miranda how to feed Penzance and the herons?"

"Come on, Miss Randy," invited Micajah, chuckling. "You'll find out that after everything else around here feeds, then the humans can."

Aunt Corinth shot him a withering look. "You know perfectly well, Micajah Chance, that the only reason you're here at all is because I broke my leg."

"Reckon I do," he said wryly. "I give you one thing, Corrie, you sure will sacrifice to get your menagerie taken care of!" With that he stalked off through the kitchen and Randy followed.

The screened porch built onto the kitchen was separate from the breezeway connecting the main house to the newer section. Breezeway and house formed two sides of a spacious yard that was closed on the other sides by a wire fence which must have sagged at one time under the weight of the vines that now seemed to hold it up.

Randy had little time to notice the large pens spaced along the fence, for as soon as she and Micajah stepped out of the main house there was a flurry of color and sound as a dozen birds converged on the back door. They all seemed possessed of long graceful necks and long legs, except for the leader, who somewhat resembled a black goose.

"Mostly egrets and herons," explained Micajah, opening an oversize refrigerator from which a fishy odor instantly swelled. "You can get acquainted in a minute, but right now could you stuff these Vitamin B-1 capsules in about a dozen fish? Like this."

Plunking a mass of medium-sized and small fish on an oil-cloth-covered high table, he opened a big jar of vitamins and stuck one down a fish's mouth.

"Ugh!" groaned Randy.

"I know," soothed Micajah. "But you'll get used to it. Redwines were always game to their last breath."

The smell of fish made Randy think she was closer to that ultimate gasp than she cared to be. It was novel and disconcerting to be assessed as one of a family with definite traits, rather than as an isolated individual. She wasn't sure if she liked the idea or not, but she did feel bound to uphold Aunt Corinth's honor.

Seizing a small fish, she poked one of the capsules down its throat, then reached for another, overcoming her squeamishness much faster than she'd dreamed she could. Must be that fine old Redwine heritage, she thought sardonically.

While she was thus employed, Micajah had begun feeding, starting with the vitamin-packed fish. When these were gone, he handed Randy a plastic pan of untreated ones.

"Smelts and mullets," he explained. "Travis buys 'em wholesale, couple hundred pounds at a time. Besides these two freezers on the porch, there's one in the spare room next to yours. Every night you leave some to thaw for next morning, and in the morning, let some thaw for the evening. You'd better give Gronker another fish so he'll let you get on to the others."

"He's the black one?"

"Yep. He's a double-crested cormorant. Got a crippled wing. Corrie's given him the run of the yard since he'll never be able to live in the wilds. Bosses the other birds, even though he's the smallest."

"Grunk!" fussed the cormorant.

Stepping out, Randy watched his hooked orange-yellow beak with some apprehension. He had gorgeous bright emerald eyes, and on closer view his arched wings looked dark brown with black scallops.

She gave this brigand his fish and moved on to join Micajah, who was passing out rations to birds as he named them.

"This one's a common egret," he said, while Randy wondered how such a beautiful graceful bird could be called common. "These are snowy egrets—their plumes are fancier, you see. They've got golden feet but their legs are black. That one you're feeding is a great blue heron."

He looked more gray than blue to Randy. He had a long black plume and head patch and more black patches on his shoulders. Accepting a fish with an eagerness that belied his aristocratic mien, he strode off on long thin legs. Next she fed a handsome black-crowned night heron with a white underbody gleaming beneath a shining greenish-black crown and back. Then she finished up with a little blue heron, darker of body than the Great Blue and with a maroon head and neck, before following Micajah to the pens, detouring around two big plastic wading pools.

"This is Witchie," he said, opening a small window through

17

which he dropped a number of small fish into a plastic pan below. "She's vicious, so don't get in pecking range without gloves."

Witchie's looks explained her name, if temperament had not. She resembled a sort of bird Frankenstein, assembled with snake neck, turkey feathers, and tortoise-like shoulders. She ceased a staccato clicking to snatch her food. Randy stared at her in fascinated horror.

"What *is* she?"

"Water turkey. Anhinga. Snakebird. Witchie was smashed up by a boat propeller but she's almost well enough to be let go." He added almost defensively, "She looks ugly here, but her kind cuts through the water like you wouldn't believe, and in the air they're mighty fine to see. Soar and spiral like hawks."

His voice softened as he moved along to the next cage. "Hi, Moses. How's the boy?"

Micajah opened the pen door and put a handful of minnows in a dish for a little blue-greenish-backed bird. "Corrie raised him from a mite—she called him Moses because the nest he was in washed up after a bad storm. He's got his feathers now, and as soon as he learns to fish, she'll leave his pen open so he can go in and out till he finally takes off altogether."

Gronker planted himself in front of Randy, demanding and getting another mullet before he let her and Micajah go inside. Micajah left one fish pan in the laundry sink and took the other, with a few mullet, through Aunt Corinth's bedroom to the bath. The door stood ajar and Randy glimpsed an astonishing sight.

Travis was kneeling on the floor, moving his head back and forth and making soft croaking noises to a cormorant, which wiggled its head and *gronked* happily in response.

Hearing Micajah, Travis rose hastily. Randy took malicious delight in his embarrassment, though she grew in her estimation for trying to entertain the invalid.

"Penzance had a broken leg," Micajah explained, giving the cormorant one fish and sliding the rest into a dish on the newspaper-spread floor. "Isn't he about ready for a pen, Travis?"

"We'll move him tomorrow," Travis said. "I've fed Penelope so I guess now it's our turn."

Ten minutes later, washed and tidied, Randy joined the

18

others at the table by the window looking out on a giant magnolia tree that shaded that whole side of the house. The stew was delicious, and Randy had never tasted anything as good as the crusty dill-flavored bread spread with fresh butter.

"What's in the coffee?" she asked, getting up to pour the pungent black brew as Travis put wedges of deep-dish rhubarb pie on their emptied bread plates.

"Chicory," said Aunt Corinth. "Do you like it?"

"It's—different," Randy said diplomatically.

"You're ruining it with cream and sugar," rumbled Micajah.

Travis laughed. "It's the only way she can swallow the stuff," he guessed with complete accuracy. "A person's got to grow up in Louisiana or East Texas to like the stuff. This won't float a spoon," he added to Randy. "So it's not what you'd call strong."

I would, thought Randy. But the tartly sweet pie with its crisp succulent pastry was a close rival to the bread in tasting pleasure. The meal was well worth a little chicory, though she resolved to get a jar of instant coffee at the first chance.

After the meal, she and her aunt gave the small birds their last feeding while the men did the dishes, and then they helped her carry the bowls and cages to the bedroom.

As she put down Ruff's cage and made a good-night kissing sound to him, Randy sighed with relief. "That's easier than getting human babies off to bed! But how does Aunt Corinth do it all?"

"She likes to," said Micajah simply.

Travis didn't speak. He only gave Randy an eloquent glance stating louder than words that of course no huckstering, money-grubbing, hired-pen flack for Quality Lumber could appreciate devotion to the Big Thicket's furred and feathered denizens.

Back in the living room, Aunt Corinth was resting in her chair, but she raised her head as Randy and the men entered. "Now," she said, fixing a steady amber gaze on Randy, "I reckon I want to hear what Travis was heckling you about, child. What kind of business are you in?"

Randy felt hot blood mounting to her face. If, as Travis accused, Quality's operations contributed to the ruin of creatures like those her aunt had succored, she didn't see how she'd be able to work on the account. But she wasn't going to accept prejudice as fact until she could judge for herself, and she wasn't going to hang her head and act guilty.

"I've got to go," said Travis, dropping a kiss on Aunt Corinth's ear. "I'll come by tomorrow if I get a chance. Want to ride along, Micajah?"

"Think I'll stay till I'm run out." Micajah slanted a ruefully adoring look at his long-wooed sweetheart. "Now that Miss Randy's here, I don't expect I'll be needed or welcome."

It was Aunt Corinth's turn to redden. "You're a fool, Micajah Chance!"

"Must be," he agreed. "Or I'd nowise have spent my life mooning over a serpent-tongued woman."

"You've spent your life rattling around the bay-galls and bogs," sniffed his lady. "Pretending to care about me just gave you an excuse not to settle down!"

Micajah twitched with outrage. "Chance men always pick one woman. If'n they can't wed her, they batch to the end of their days. Dang it, Corrie Redwine, you know that!"

"Horsefeathers!"

"Good night," said Travis, and exited with a stern, rather puzzled look at Randy.

Deciding she might as well describe her work to her aunt to divert her attention from the ruffled Micajah, Randy sat down on the rug near her aunt's footstool and told about her two years at Summit.

"This Greg Hathaway," mused Aunt Corinth. "You're in love with him?"

That morning Randy would have said yes. Now New York, Greg, her neat, empty, modern apartment, the job at Summit—all seemed worlds, if not lives, away. "I—I—we're sort of engaged."

Why did Travis Lee's thin brown face keep clouding her image of Greg?

"Do you love him?" Aunt Corinth persisted.

"Of course!" Randy's peculiar uneasiness and discontent made her speak vehemently. "I haven't dated anyone else in over a year. He's intelligent, has a good sense of humor, stays in shape, is dependable—"

"A Boy Scout is loyal," Aunt Corinth said, deadpan.

Randy laughed in spite of herself and then felt cross about it. "I suppose romances always sound ridiculous if one tries to explain them," she said pointedly. She, after all, hadn't kept a devoted suitor dangling for over forty years.

Micajah chortled heartily, and Aunt Corinth joined him,

rather sheepishly. Then Aunt Corinth put Greg aside, furrowing her brow. "So you're supposed to do a glamor job on Quality?"

"I don't have to," Randy said. "But Greg thought I might turn up some good angles." She stopped and swallowed. "Is Quality as destructive as Travis Lee says?"

Aunt Corinth's eyes blazed, then smoldered, as if she were telling herself to count ten. "You have a look where they've been," she said.

Just then Randy was knocked off balance by a hairy missile that lunged into her lap. As she gasped and stared into the eager whiskered face, Penelope flopped over, waved her webbed paws, and made a very human giggling sound, obviously begging to be tickled.

Randy obliged, cautiously at first. Then, as the otter reacted like an exceedingly intelligent and mischievous puppy, Randy grew bolder and scratched behind the small neat ears, then rubbed Penelope's belly till the otter decided to visit Aunt Corinth. Nestling in between woman and chair arm, Penelope drowsed off on her back, paws crossed on her chest.

The room was suddenly quiet.

Aunt Corinth sighed. "Micajah?" Her tone was shy.

"Corrie?" His warm hazel eyes lit up, and Randy felt exasperated with her aunt for not better rewarding his long devotion.

"Do you still play the dulcimer?"

Everybody was blushing tonight, everyone but that sanctimonious Travis Lee, for Micajah turned crimson right up to his silver thatch.

"Might come back to me—if you wanted to hear."

"Try. Please."

The wiry little man went over to the fireplace and picked up the dulcimer, looked about, and took down a quill from the mantel. He tuned and tightened the strings, strummed a bit, hummed under his breath, and finally began to play, singing along in a sweet, somewhat rusty voice.

Randy was sure that once he used to play for her aunt like this, when his hair was bright yellow and her figure was less like a scrawny boy's. How long had it been?

"Greensleeves," "The Woods So Wild," "Bonnie Sweet Robin"—songs brought over from Elizabethan England, changed in the Blue Ridge and Smoky Mountains, filtered on to the Piney Woods of Texas.

21

Way down in the valley in a lonesome place,
Where the wild birds do sing and their notes
    do increase ...

And then Micajah drew up a bench close to Corinth Redwine's chair. She looked flustered, as if she would have
moved away if the cast hadn't been a hindrance. But her russet eyes, like his hazel ones, looked young and eager.

Entranced as she was with the old songs, Randy felt like
an interloper. "I could listen all night," she said, rising. "But
I'm tired. Two hours later than your time, you know." She
thanked Micajah again for helping liberate her car, then
kissed her aunt's lifted cheek and started for her room, Micajah's song reaching after her.

Wake up, wake up, darlin' Corrie,
And go get me my gun.
I ain't no hand for trouble
But I'll die before I'll run.

The Chances must always have played a mean dulcimer,
Randy thought, smiling. Micajah might be taking some advantage of Aunt Corinth's weakened state, but Randy found
herself wishing him well as she readied herself for bed. He
was a kind, considerate, thoughtful man, gentle and tender.

Micajah was not the least like that hard-bitten cynical Travis Lee, who had a housckeeper, not a wife. *He* probably
hated women. Her association with Quality doubtless just
gave him an excuse to be obnoxious.

And he might come by tomorrow! Well, she was fore-
warned. Tomorrow she'd be ready for him. Tomorrow ...

4

Since she suspected that ravenous baby birds woke with dawn's first light, Randy had set her travel alarm for five. She woke to its raucous whir and started to choke it to silence, then suddenly remembered where she was and why.

Yawning prodigiously, she stumbled up, splashed cold water on her face till the worst drowsiness faded, and dressed quickly, glad that she'd packed mostly jeans and washable tops, though she certainly hadn't expected to wind up in a birds' and beasties' emergency ward.

As she entered the breezeway, there was a dark flash through a swinging flap near the door, and Penelope landed at her feet. The otter lifted her long sleek neck and chuckled, and Randy scratched her behind the ears.

"You're a devil, aren't you?" she chided. "Lurking in ambush, scaring respectable people! No, I can't rub your tummy now, you sensuous, sinuous baby! The birds must be starving."

Aunt Corinth, aided by crutches, was balancing herself like a stork in her bathroom, *gronking* to Penzance. The older woodpeckers were thumping away like a mob of different drummers, and the smaller ones were cheeping as they climbed about their mixing bowls.

"Shall I give them their first feed here and then move them?" Randy called.

"Good idea," said her aunt, hobbling to the bed. "I can do the babies if you'll mix their food first."

Half an hour later, all the birds were fed and settled by Aunt Corinth's chair. Penelope had feasted on leftover stew and fish and was entertaining herself with a squeaky rubber mouse. Randy went out to feed the backyard birds and found with relief that Micajah was already there, with the "Yard Birds" fed, although Gronker was demanding more fishy tribute before he would let her join Micajah at Witchie's pen.

Giving the cormorant highwayman a mullet, Randy looked to Micajah for directions. "Would you stuff a minnow with a vitamin capsule and feed it to Moses?" he asked. "Then we'll begin his education."

That education proved to be live minnows swimming in a small plastic tub. At first Moses eyed them in bafflement. The minnows he was used to lay still. What was wrong with these perverse creatures?

His first few attempts to fish were in vain, but soon he was gulping the minnows down. Micajah gave a satisfied nod. "Few more days should pretty well teach him. Then we'll leave his pen open so he can wander around. Next step is to open his pen on the outside fence so he can start exploring easy but still feed here when he needs to. Corrie tries to let the birds judge for themselves when they're ready to fend in the wilds."

Gronker claimed a last mullet as Randy edged past him. "What a little pirate! How will he get along with Penzance?"

"Penzance will stay in a pen till he's ready to fly," said Micajah. "Travis can move him if he stops by today. I'm not getting cozier than needs be with either water turkeys or cormorants."

"Travis seems to know a lot about birds," ventured Randy, hoping Micajah would tell her more about his arrogant but fascinating companion.

"He's pretty fair at patching wings and legs," granted the old hunter. "You want to help Corrie with the bitsies or feed Penzance?"

"Why don't you help her?" Randy suggested.

He gave her a grateful, measuring look. "You're a nice gal," he said. "Maybe in the wrong job. But a sweet lady. Don't let old Travis ruffle your feathers. He and Corrie are mighty like. Used to having their own way and bound to have their say, even if it harelips every dog in the county."

"What?" gasped Randy, dazed.

Micajah was already gone. Randy got a few more small fish out of the porch refrigerator and went along to Penzance.

She fed him, took up the soiled papers, put clean ones down, and when he *gronked* wistfully, looking up at her with softly radiant green eyes, Randy got down on her knees and waggled her head at him, imitating his gentle sounds.

24

"Not bad for a beginning *Phalacrocorax auritus*," drawled a deep voice.

Even in her chagrin, Randy took care not to startle the happy cormorant, letting her head wag gradually to a stop before she rose with all possible dignity, which wasn't much.

"Are you moving Penzance to a cage, Mr. Lee?"

"Soon as his breakfast settles a bit." The gray eyes were almost friendly. "Why don't we first-name it, Miranda?"

"I'd like that, Travis." To her embarrassment, the name came out like a caress. "I'd better help Micajah get breakfast," she added hastily, staring at Travis' top shirt button. "Mmmm! He's already got the coffee on. Doesn't it smell grand?"

She fled, sensing Travis lounging amusedly behind her. Micajah was already frying eggs and stirring oatmeal, so Randy made toast and helped Travis set the table with a blue crockery pitcher full of milk, honey welling from a comb, strawberry preserves, and marmalade.

Aunt Corinth hobbled in, sitting by the window with her foot up on a stool Travis got for her. Filling blue bowls with steaming oatmeal, Randy brought them to the table, while Micajah brought a platter of eggs and Travis poured black chicory coffee.

"These are the best eggs I ever had," Randy praised.

Micajah looked pleased but said modestly, "Reckon it's because they're so fresh. Maybe you don't get 'em like that in New York."

"Do you keep chickens?" Randy asked her aunt.

"Great day in the morning, no!" cut in Micajah. "Corrie's not going to feed and fuss after anything that might be worth its keep!"

"As if your passel of hounds was," she retorted. "Travis keeps me in milk, butter, and eggs, Miranda. Cash can be pretty short around here, so Travis is forever getting paid in dairy stuff, or a ham or such. Bet he's got more pickles and mayhaw jelly than any ten families in the county, even though he's always giving food away."

Travis fidgeted as if he'd been accused of something shameful. "People feel better when they pay. What I do with the results is my own business." He grinned. "You won't see me parting with any white lightning or dandelion wine."

"White lightning?" asked Randy.

"Moonshine," explained Micajah. "Homemade corn liquor.

Make it better in the Big Thicket than anywhere else in the whole United States."

He sounded so expert that Randy decided not to ask for more details than she'd be comfortable knowing. Just in case the "revenooers" turned up. Good grief, was all this really happening? Or would she wake up tomorrow in her beige, white, and black bedroom and have to dash for her bus?

"What business are you in?" she asked Travis, unable to restrain her curiosity any longer. He was dressed and looked like a backwoodsman, but his speech was educated and there was an indefinable something about him that hinted at an ability to fit in almost anywhere.

Not that Travis Lee would fit in; he just would stay himself, so naturally and so strongly that groups would eddy around him as waters past an immovable rock. Randy had always thought of Greg as being dominant and forceful. And so he was, in terms of ambition and thrusting forward. Greg's power was like a strong current. But if the current struck a rock it would lose its force, though in centuries, if not diverted, it might wear the rock away.

"I'm a doctor," Travis said.

"A doctor?" Randy echoed. "A—a veterinarian?"

He laughed, not the least offended. "Sometimes it seems like that," he admitted. "But I've got my license to set bones, hand out pills, and give people lots of advice they don't follow."

"Best dang doctor in the Thicket!" praised Micajah. "Why, they wanted him up at Mayo's, and big clinics down in Houston are always pestering him to join up with them. Don't make any mistake about it, Miss Randy, Travis doesn't need to stay here and take his pay in sausage and fruitcakes and shelled hickory nuts."

"No way I could get that kind of thing in Houston," Travis grinned. "Guess I'm too lazy for city practice."

"Lazy!" snorted Aunt Corinth. "You wade bogs at midnight to deliver babies for folks who haven't paid yet for your bringin' their last one. Run a free well-baby clinic and nutrition and home-nursing classes—"

"Proves I'm lazy," shrugged Travis. "If people know how to keep well they don't bother me so much." He glanced at his watch. "Even so, the office opens at nine. Got just time to move Penzance, Miss Corinth."

"Good! He's the sweetest-natured cormorant I ever knew, but I'll be glad to get my bathroom back." The small red-

26

haired woman pushed up from her chair and collected her crutches. "Micajah, if you'll bring me the hamburger and water, I can feed the little birds. Miranda, why don't you help Travis and learn how to handle a cormorant?"

This bit of knowledge might prove rather exotic once she got back to New York. Still, Randy watched with interest as Travis pulled on garden gloves and picked up a towel.

"Penzance seems so tame," she said. "Do you think he'd bite?"

"Don't think where anhingas and cormorants are concerned," advised Travis. "You can lose an eye or need a lot of stitches as the price of letting go of their bills for just one second. Always wear gloves and hang onto that bill till you can get out of range."

In the door of the bathroom, Travis got down on all fours, wiggled his head, and *gronked* at the delighted Penzance, who croaked back and waggled his head. Once a rapport was well established, Travis, still making cormorant sounds, clasped Penzance's yellow-orange bill firmly and lifted him gently in the towel. Penzance seemed startled, but after a brief huffing of his wings he didn't struggle.

Randy hurried to open the doors. A partially roofed pen beyond Moses' was open, and Travis carefully deposited the bird on the clean sand there. There was a small doghouse for further shade and a large plastic dishpan of clean water. Penzance hunkered on the sand for a moment. Such a lot of space it must seem after weeks in the bathroom!

"Won't be long till he can go," said Travis. "I hate to get a broken leg in a swimming bird. Breaks at a joint can almost never mend so that the bird can survive on its own. Penzance's break, luckily, was above the joint. When his strength comes back, he'll be good as new."

The herons and egrets were mostly strolling about, wading in the swimming pools, although some had retired for a bit of contemplative exclusivity into their cages. Gronker bustled around in front of Travis and Randy, his lame wing making him list slightly. With his bright orange bill and pouch, emerald eyes, and gleaming black feathers, he resembled a swashbuckling, somewhat tipsy buccaneer.

He was almost under Randy's feet as she started up the steps. Without thinking, she patted his head. There was a black and orange flash as his long neck slewed around. Randy yelped and snatched up the offending hand, which was already dripping blood. Gronker retreated, eying them belligerently.

"Get in here," urged Travis, almost lifting her onto the porch. "Here, drip over the sink. That's good, gets out the germs. Stay right there and I'll douse you with antiseptic." He produced a plastic bottle from the shelf above and poured a stinging liquid on her hand. "Always use this on any nips or scratches," he advised. "There. You were lucky. Wear a stick-on bandage for a day or two, and all you'll have to remember Gronker by will be a little dimple on the side of your hand."

"I'll remember him!" Randy vowed. She blinked away the tears that had come involuntarily at the shock. "How stupid of me! And right after you wore gloves to move Penzance!"

"One bite is worth a million words," laughed Travis, but he wasn't being superior or malicious.

Randy wondered if he could tell how her pulse raced at his touch even though he was deftly professional as he supported her injured hand and applied a second wash of antiseptic. "A nip in time saves nine," he joked. "You've learned a lesson that might have cost you an eye or finger."

Opening a tin of adhesive bandages, he found one to fit the small wound, applying it with a thoroughness that sent funny little shivers chasing through her, completely anesthetizing any twinges from the bite.

He didn't release her hand, though. He seemed to draw her closer, and for once his gray eyes were neither mocking nor accusing. "When you were little," he said, in a tone that was soft yet still had power to it, a leashed force that made her breath come fast while a sweet tremulous dizziness weakened her, "did your mother ever kiss a hurt to make it well?"

Randy had to laugh. "I wouldn't stop crying till she did! It was—a kind of magic."

"I could use some magic myself," he said.

Holding her—as much with a controlled but imperative hunger in his eyes as with his long tough-muscled arms—he bent his head. His mouth was smiling as it met hers, gentle, almost teasing, before the kiss changed, grew urgent, seeking, demanding, shaking her to the center of her being. Greg had never made her feel like this—all soft, yielding, and floating while fires ignited in her blood.

At first she tried feebly to push him away, but as Travis' hard, tender, wooing, insistent mouth awakened in her sensations she had never guessed could be, her hands moved up around his neck as if possessed of a will of their own.

She heard a distant, faraway ringing, but it was Travis, not she, who stepped back regretfully, ending that timeless, limitless moment.

"May be one of my impatient patients," he apologized, glancing at his watch. "I've got to run, damn it! Randy—"

She would never know what he started to say, for just then Micajah poked his head through the door. "Call for you, Miss Randy. Long distance, person-to-person. Must be your boss."

If she had suddenly broken out in green and cerise spots, Travis couldn't have moved off faster. "He must want to know how you're coming along on your gold-washing of Quality." Travis' voice was freighted with scorn.

He held the door open for her with exaggerated courtesy. Randy sailed through, head high but with a slow spreading pain in her heart which felt as if it had developed a thousand aching, stinging little fractures.

How could he kiss her like that, as if he cared about her, and then be so mean? He followed her through the house, and it was like being stalked by a policeman.

"If you've got any ethics, you'll let me show you a few things before you tout that gang of forest-butchers." Travis' voice was lowered to reach only her ears as she paused in the corner by the phone stand. "Think about it. I'll be back this evening."

He called a good-bye to Aunt Corinth and went out the door as Randy picked up the phone, so shaken and confused that she didn't even know whether or not she wanted it to be Greg.

5

"Is something wrong?" demanded Greg before she could complete her faltering greeting.

"No! No—everything's fine."

"You sound funny."

Randy gulped and took a couple of long soothing breaths. "I just rushed in from the porch," she explained. "How are things with you?"

When Greg wanted to know something, he didn't drop the subject until he was satisfied. "I miss you," he said. "But before I go into full-color wide-screen, didn't I hear you talking to a man?"

"It was the doctor." True enough. So why did it sound mendacious even to her?

"Oh." Greg's first relief was followed by suspicion. "It sounded as if he were muttering sweet somethings in your ear."

"He certainly wasn't! He thinks Quality's operation here is a disaster and keeps goading me about that."

"Tell the old goat to get stuck in your aunt's plaster cast," snorted Greg, and Randy could picture the gleam of battle in his eye. "Quality employs a lot of people down there. Bet they're more interested in paychecks than all that ecological garbage."

"All the same—"

"Let's not fight, darling, not on long distance rates." He chuckled, apparently in a better humor. "I was hoping your aunt would say you'd missed me so much that you were already on your way back to New York."

Actually, Randy hadn't had time to miss anybody. Besides, Travis Lee had a way of infiltrating her thoughts even when she was trying hard to forget that such a lean, brown, brash, competent, arrogant man existed.

"Don't try to sweet-talk me out of my first vacation in two years," she chided laughingly. This was the busiest part of

Greg's day. He *must* wish she were back. "I'm staying my full month! Maybe longer, if Aunt Corinth's still in her cast."

"Damn it, let her hire a nurse!"

"She can't, Greg. Not for the herons and cormorants and egrets and woodpeckers—"

"Are you crazy?" he interrupted. "What the hell's she got down there, a zoo?"

Randy explained.

"A heron hospital!" Greg exploded. "An egret emergency ward! Bide-a-Wee Motel for the Mangled. You mean the old girl lured you down there to take care of her Noah's Ark and you're really standing still for it?"

"I'm not standing still."

"I'll bet you're not!" he said darkly. "It'll take you a week to recover once you're allegedly back at work."

That smarted. Especially after the skipped vacations, the nights and weekends she'd worked even before there was any hint of romance between them just because she knew the business was so important to him that she wanted it to succeed! Tears sprang to her eyes.

Blinking angrily, she said in an icy tone, "If you'd like to hire someone to replace me, Greg, go right ahead. I'm sure I can find another job when I'm through down here."

There was a shocked silence at the other end. "I'm sorry, honey." Greg's voice was rueful before it switched to that coaxing little-boy humility that always had power to melt her wrath or hurt. "You *must* be tired. Lord, angel, I know what you've put into Summit. I'd never have let you work so hard except that—well, I've figured it was for you, too. Forgive me?"

"Oh, forget it," Randy said. "Sorry I was on edge."

"No wonder, with all those birds and beasties," Greg said caressingly. "Stay as long as you think you should, sweet, I won't complain—though I may very well come down and drag you off when my endurance cracks! But you just remember one thing: your next job is to be my wife."

Strange. That thought had made her happy yesterday. Now it was almost threatening. She must still be feeling the effects of the trip and time lag.

Time lag? Unbidden, Travis' gray eyes probed her and his mouth curled with disdain.

"Love me?" Greg was saying.

"Y-y-yes." Of course she did—she couldn't have been mistaken for a whole year, could she?

"My God, Randy, you don't sound very impassioned!"

"I—I—a neighbor's dropped in to see Aunt Corinth."

"Oh." Greg sounded relieved and disappointed at the same time. "You're in the room with them and can't talk freely?"

"Yes."

"Isn't there an extension?"

"I'm sure there's not."

He sighed resignedly. "Then I'll have to talk for both of us. Let's see now: what do I want you to say to me?" He imitated her voice with a degree of accuracy that made her laugh. "Greg, lover, I dream of you by night and long for you by day and think of you every time I toss a fish to a bird. When I squint up at the moon through the magnolias—"

"Oh, hush!" begged Randy, with a vexed chuckle.

"If you don't like my fabrications, you'd better come up with something better. You can write, sweetheart, since the phone seems to be in the middle of Big Thicket Grand Central Station."

"I'll write," she promised.

"Every day?"

"Greg! The birds have to be fed every half hour!"

Astonished quiet. "Around the clock?" he demanded.

"Daylight."

"I see. Well, you can scriven a few lines at night, even so."

"I'll try, Greg. But emergencies may come up, and you must remember that we have to eat as well as the birds."

"I should have married you before I let you wander off down there," he brooded. "You'll meet some brawny Cajun Adonis who'll help you caretake those ridiculous birds and I'll be forsaken. Hey!" From the sudden energy in his voice Randy knew he had thought of something connected with business. "If you're that tied down, when are you going to look over Quality's operation?"

Randy thought of Travis Lee's last challenge. "One of the neighbors can probably fill in when it's really necessary."

"I don't see why they couldn't have filled in completely rather than you having to chase off to the bayous," grumbled Greg.

"My aunt doesn't like to impose," said Randy, glancing to where that lady and Micajah were absorbed in their own conversation. Randy could, she realized, speak as intimately as she wished to Greg. But the truth was that she didn't wish. Not just then.

"How is Sue?"

He sounded surprised. "Why, fine, I suppose. She looks okay. Got to dash, I've got three calls waiting. I'll phone again, though it doesn't seem I'm going to get much soul food. Do write a few fond words, and remember, you're my girl."

"Thanks for calling," she said automatically, knowing how inadequate it sounded even before Greg's ironically aloof tone reproached her.

"Don't mention it." He hung up abruptly.

Randy stood holding the dead phone for a few seconds, thoroughly befuddled. She couldn't blame Greg for being irritated, but she was annoyed with him, too. It was, after all, her vacation, her aunt, and her life, when it came to that.

Maybe that was the trouble. When she stopped to think about it, her life had been pretty much absorbed into Greg's, especially during this past year of engagement when it was hard to tell where her personal life ended and business began. She was good at the work and enjoyed it, and Greg's magnetism and drive had swept her along. But now, removed from his physical territory and the hectic, perpetually goal-setting atmosphere of the office, she sensed faint stirrings of rebellion.

Greg just assumed that she would glamorize Quality. And she also suspected that much of his discomfort at her absence was because he now had to cope with many of the small, trifling but time-consuming problems that she had always taken care of because they tried his patience.

If Sue was smart—and she was—she'd upgrade her skills a bit and make Greg see her as something besides the intelligence running a typewriter. Sue deserved the chance, Randy told herself. But she had to admit that she'd recover should Sue take over all her former functions.

That didn't seem a proper thought for a person in love. It was one thing to make the best of a romantic disaster once it occurred, but to comtemplate such an adjustment without great distress seemed horrifyingly pragmatic.

I do love Greg, Randy assured herself. It's just that all my New York life seems unreal right now.

"That your young man?" inquired Aunt Corinth as Randy put down the receiver.

"Yes."

"Did he have bad news?"

"No."

Aunt Corinth let out an exasperated breath. "Then what

are you so down in the mouth about?" Her amber eyes grew concerned. "Do you miss him badly, child? I'm afraid I've been a selfish old woman, but I didn't know——"

Randy shook her head. "It's not that." Crossing to her aunt, she took her hands and dropped a kiss on her cheek. "It's more than time we got away from each other for a while."

"I can manage if you need to go back," lied Aunt Corinth gallantly.

"I'm not going back till my vacation's over," said Randy. Sinking on the floor by her aunt's chair, she smiled at the diminutive woodpeckers who were tapping out a chorus on their bits of wood and cages. "It's just that Greg seems sure I'll be able to write a lot of good things about Quality, and I'm beginning to wonder."

"After one look you won't wonder," said Micajah.

"That bad?" Randy frowned.

"Seeing is believing." Aunt Corinth stroked her niece's hair. "Will your boss-beau be in a huff if you don't sing Quality's praises?"

"He'd be angry, but I don't think he'd fire me or break our engagement." Randy sighed and nibbled at her lip. "The snag is that it's a huge account. He'll do it, even if I won't."

"And you feel that because you're more—more linked with the decision-maker than most employees that you'd share the blame for misleading the public?"

Randy nodded.

Aunt Corinth made a soothing sound, the same as she did to small birds that were too dazed to feed. "Don't fret about it now, dear. Thunder's not rain." Without trying for any finesse, she changed the subject abruptly. "What do you think of that quilt on the frame?"

Though she had noticed it upon arrival, Randy had been too busy to pay the stunning creation the attention it deserved. Crossing to the frame, she gazed in wonder at the appliquéd tree that filled the center. On every branch perched a different bird—cardinal, bluejay, woodpecker, lark, owl, robin, plus others she couldn't name.

Artfully entwined amid vines and leaves making the border were many animals: deer, fox, wolf, otter, opossum, skunk, bear. And here were the larger birds: heron, eagle, hawk, cormorant, crane, anhinga, turkey. These were worked in natural colors upon a snowy white muslin background.

An overall design which looked rather like a flowing

feather was marked on in pencil, and the part held by the frame was being sewn with tiny green running stitches.

"You do this by hand?" asked Randy, astounded and almost terrified at the number of stitches that would have to be made before the quilt was done. "Why, you must have spent years on it!"

"It is taking a fair amount of time," granted Aunt Corinth. "But spring is the busiest time with birds, and again in the fall when hunters cut loose at everything that moves. Winters I spend many an hour sewing away. Do you still have your baby quilt?"

How could Randy have forgotten that blue quilt with a rabbit family playing all over it? Now she remembered, with the lump that rose in her throat when she remembered life with her parents back when everything had seemed so safe and warm and happy.

"It's stored in a cedar chest of treasures," she said. "And you must have made that rose wreath quilt my parents were so proud of. I saved it, too, though I sold most of the furniture. Only a few pieces would fit in my apartment."

"Don't see how folks can live in a room or two like that," said Micajah. "No place to spill over or add onto, the way it was done with this house and plenty like it."

"That's a city," Aunt Corinth said. "But I'm glad you kept the rose wreath quilt, Miranda. It was my wedding gift to your parents."

That sounded a vague memory in Randy, shrouded by childhood acceptance of things as they are, as if they could never have been different. "I'm sure mother or father told me that," Randy said. "I just didn't remember."

"You saved the quilt, that's the main thing." Aunt Corinth's tone was brisk. "Shall I tell you a secret?"

"Oh, please!" begged Randy, intrigued.

"That's a bride quilt yonder."

"Really? What a marvelous present! Whom is it for?"

"You." The fiery curls bobbed as Aunt Corinth nodded in satisfaction at Randy's surprise. "I started the quilt last spring when the mayhaws were ripening and had the pattern set by time to gather hickory nuts. Dawned on me you were twenty-three and any day I might hear you were getting married, so I'd best be getting a move on. When are you and this Greg tying the knot? I'd like to do all the work myself, more personal that way, but if the date's soon, I can get the Muscateen Free Will Baptist Church Ladies' Society to finish the background stitching."

"Oh, you can't give it to me!" Randy protested, absolutely numb when she thought of the hours of painstaking work. "It's a—a treasure, an heirloom."

"Isn't that what wedding gifts should be?" Aunt Corinth eyed her sternly. "You're my closest relative, dear. Ephesus was too busy gadding about to have children, and poor Sidon vanished decades ago in the jungles. Now when's your wedding?"

"We haven't set a time."

Aunt Corinth's reddish eyebrows squiggled. "How long have you been engaged?"

"About a year, more or less."

"About? More or less?" Aunt Corinth took the lid off the bird food mixed fresh that morning, and Micajah and Randy began to help with the feeding. "Doesn't sound as if you're in a feverish rush."

"May run in the family," observed Micajah drily.

Aunt Corinth blushed but returned to her probing. "Your young man, child. He wants to stay in New York?"

With a startled laugh, Randy found that she couldn't imagine him anyplace else. "I'm not sure Greg believes there is any other city."

Aunt Corinth's face fell. "Stands to reason. Not much advertising around Muscateen."

Had the older woman cherished a hope that Randy might come back to live in the area? Even though there was no basis for such an assumption, Randy felt guilty and was glad to fix her attention on the gaping little mouths.

But Aunt Corinth was not one to let her hopes smother in genteel silence. As soon as all the hungry feathered crew were fed, she leaned back in her chair, grimaced at the awkward cast, and fixed her niece with lambent fox eyes.

"I plan to leave this home place to you, Miranda. What are you going to do with it?"

6

Dumbfounded, Miranda stared helplessly at her aunt. "Don't do that!" she cried, once she was capable of speech. "This house needs someone to live in it. The way it's been added to and changed from the first one-room cabin is—well, it's a history of the Redwines, actually, a kind of living record of this part of the country. It shouldn't belong to someone in New York."

"You're the last Redwine."

"That's not my fault," blurted Randy.

Micajah looked grimly at the woman who had refused him since their springtime years. "You should have had your own young 'uns, Corrie."

"Not if it meant compromising my principles." When her withering glance had no obvious effect on him, Aunt Corinth turned again to Randy. "Look, my dear," she said plaintively. "I suppose I should tell you the truth."

That I'm not my father's child? Randy thought wildly. That female Redwines carry some malignant congenital malady? That I've been exposed to some swamp fever which will quarantine me here forever?

With the air of one admitting to villainous dynastic plotting, Aunt Corinth lifted her chin. "It's true enough that I'd have a hard time taking care of all the birds with this damnable cast with just Travis and Micajah's help, but I could have managed—though I surely hate to be obligated to a *hunter*. The real reason I asked you to come was to see if you were a fitting heir, and if you were, to persuade you to settle here sometime."

"I'm not a fitting heir, Aunt Corinth. Not for all this." Randy's gesture indicated the old fireplace, the wonderful quilt, the old majestic trees that beyond the house clearing. "It needs someone to take care of it, to love it . . . Even if I could live here, I wouldn't know how to look after things."

"You didn't know how to feed a bird till you got here,"

37

pointed out Aunt Corinth. She patted Randy's bandaged hand. "Now you've learned to be wary. If you come back to it, the home place will teach you all you need to know."

"But, Aunt Corinth—"

"I've made up my mind. You'll inherit."

Randy's temper heated. She was attracted to this old house, beguiled by its mellow, time-gentled peace; she admired her aunt though it would have seemed impertinent to love her so soon and without specific permission. But she was not going to allow these new feelings and her iron-willed aunt to trick her into agreeing to an undertaking that would quite literally change her whole life.

"I can't keep you from leaving your property to whomever you choose," she said. "But you must understand that I'd probably have to sell it."

Aunt Corinth stiffened with angry dismay. Then she smiled and shook her head. "I'll bet you won't."

"You could lose."

"I doubt it."

Hard-headed! Stubborn! Willful, cantankerous, obstinate! Mulish, bull-headed—

Micajah's mournful watchword interrupted Randy's silent litany. "The Redwines were always set in their ways. No stopping them once they get the bit between their teeth."

"I'm a Redwine, too," said Randy.

Aunt Corinth chuckled smugly. "That's what I'm counting on. Make up your mind to it, girl. Soon or late, you'll have to decide what to do with this house and land. Sure, you can sell it for a good price to the lumber people. They've pestered me for years. But they'll knock this cabin down, break up the foundations, and start on the trees. By the time they finish there won't need to be any shelter for birds and wild things here because there won't be any. Just rows and rows of slash pine with herbicides to kill other trees and plants, and pesticides to kill off pine borer beetles."

"Don't!" Randy cried, "You make it sound like the end of the world."

"It is, in a way," said Micajah.

The rest of the morning and afternoon passed in busy quiet as Randy took advantage of Micajah's presence to let him keep her aunt company and help feed the baby birds while she gave the bathroom a cleaning that banished the last whiff of Penzance. Then she dust-mopped and dusted and mopped the kitchen.

Travis and Micajah had kept the sink free of dirty dishes, and the wastebaskets had been emptied into the incinerator beyond the fence, but Randy suspected that her aunt was getting the fidgets over the neglected areas. Travis must have brought by fresh salad things that morning, for the refrigerator crisper was full.

For lunch, Randy concocted a huge green salad with slivers of ham and cheese and sliced hard-boiled eggs. Comparing the foods in the kitchen with her skills, she stirred up a tomato sauce that would simmer with a bay leaf all afternoon, the last hour with browned hamburger, and go over the whole-wheat spaghetti she found in a tall glass jar with other staples such as rice, lentils, beans, and dried peas.

With the house at least surface-tidied and dinner on the way, Randy sighed and stretched. In the distance she heard Micajah picking out a song for Aunt Corinth on the dulcimer. Randy decided that she had earned a shower. Travis might be along any minute. Even if he was impossibly critical, she found that she didn't want to look a wreck when he came. Not that a person could dress up when she had to feed a bunch of egrets and herons and cormorants!

Crossing the breezeway, Randy breathed in the sweetness of the magnolia blooms, the rich heady blossoming of early summer. It was a lovely time to be here. Of course fall must be gorgeous, too, a blaze of changing beech, gum, and oak against cypress and piness. And winter!

Wouldn't it be lovely to see the snow blanket all this? And learn the tracks of the animals who'd cross the clearing? And sit by the flickering fire in the generations-old hearth, listening to Micajah sing and helping Aunt Corinth stitch that magnificent bride quilt?

Then spring again, new leaves, baby birds and beasts, flowers everywhere, and the breeze so fragrant . . .

The screen door was just a bit ajar. Had she left the solid one open? Randy was somewhat nervous of snakes and spiders, and she thought that she had closed the door quite firmly before, though it stood wide open now.

Gingerly, she stepped inside, watching the floor. No snake had taken up homestead rights, but a long, sleek, dark brown body lay on its back in the middle of the rug, bedecked with a slinky green nylon jersey dressing gown Randy had left on the chair. One sleeve trailed, Greek fashion, over Penelope's

39

shoulder, and she clasped a dusting powder puff to her bosom.

The pose of a Lily Maid of Astolat, sweet-sadly dead for love, coupled with otter whiskers and stubby webbed feet, sent Randy into fits of laughter.

"You little wretch! Have you spilled dusting powder all over the place?" She peered in the bathroom, was relieved to find that Penelope, with her clever paws, had taken the puff and let the powder be.

Penelope wriggled and giggled, dark eyes glowing, so that Randy couldn't be vexed. Sitting down by the funny little beast, she gathered her in her arms, flowing robe and all, and tickled her belly while Penelope shivered and chuckled with delight.

"Why, Miss Redwine!" came a deep amused voice from the door. "Still playing with dolls?"

He had an absolute gift, did Travis Lee, for catching her in absurd situations. Scrambling up, Randy salvaged the jade-green robe, but Penelope hung on to the puff and would not be parted from such a delectably soft and fluffy plaything.

"All right," conceded Randy. "I don't suppose I want odor of otter added to my Chantilly anyway!"

Penelope scuttled and skidded out the screen door to Travis, flaunting her trophy. He scooped her up and tickled her under the chin while she nestled against him, looking like a cross between a seal and dachshund.

"You're a great gal," he told her, setting her down with a last pat. "But that powder will never smell the same on you as it does on someone who isn't addicted to feasting on fish heads she's tucked under a chair."

His gray eyes touched Randy in an intimate, caressing way that made her blush. Was he, too, remembering that kiss? Randy felt a pulse hammering in her throat. She felt utterly exposed and vulnerable.

What was happening? She loved Greg, didn't she? Then what was this strange wild melting Travis could cause just by watching her, smiling in that lazy mocking way? And why should she feel such relief that he seemed to have shed the anger that was on him when he left that morning during Greg's call?

"Come here, Miranda."

She stood rather helplessly, still holding the robe. "I—I want to have a shower."

"Seems rather a waste right before feeding time," he said.

"Never mind, I'm in no rush tonight. Don't keep office hours on Saturday."

With that, he crossed the breezeway with Penelope, who proudly flaunted her trophy. Randy hurried into the shower, found another puff for the scented powder, and twenty minutes later, after giving the meat sauce a stir, joined Travis at stuffing vitamin capsules into fish.

"Stuff smells a little different on you than on Penny," he said, sniffing comically. "Micajah's already given Moses his practice minnows. How's your hand?"

"Fine but the bandage is a nuisance. Can't I take it off?"

"I'll check it for you later. It's better to protect open cuts while you're handling fish and fooling around with birds."

Gronker barricaded the steps. If he remembered his ungrateful attack of the morning, he didn't show it. Instead he hoisted his wings and croaked until Randy gave him a mullet. Moses was spearing fish from his wading pool, well over this morning's bewilderment at the way the minnows moved.

Witchie clicked chatteringly at Travis. "Maybe we'll let you go tomorrow," he said to her. "If you're feeling peppy enough to fuss, you could be ready to fend for yourself again."

Eyeing him with malevolent gleaming eyes, Witchie retired, still clattering, to the edge of her pen. Penzance greeted his human friends with a happy *gronk* and tried to get a head-wiggling game going, but Travis gave him his fish and said briskly, "Now that you're out of solitary, old fellow, you can dream up your own entertainment."

Penzance looked so desolate that Randy, lingering, knelt to croak and waggle for a few minutes. She had a couple of fish left in her pan and turned to find Gronker gulping down the last one. He was already so full that the tail wouldn't quite go down his throat but stuck out of the side of his mouth.

"Won't he choke?" Randy cried in fright.

Travis turned from Moses' pen to stare at Gronker, who waddled away without any apparent distress. "He seems to be okay," Travis said. "It should slide down as soon as the little robber digests his regular meal. Let's disinfect your bite and eat ourselves. I'm starving, and whatever that is on the stove sure smells great!"

Washed and disinfected, with the hand pronounced fit for use without a bandage tomorrow, Randy heaped spaghetti on a big platter and ladled the meat sauce over it, while Travis

41

put together a salad. Micajah had set the table along with all the trimmings, and soon, once Aunt Corinth had been seated in her place by the window, they were dining heartily.

Randy's spaghetti was praised, not only in words but also by generous seconds and even a third portion for Micajah. When Aunt Corinth and Micajah went back to the living room and feeding the small woodpeckers, Travis washed dishes while Randy dried.

They were standing close together because of the tight corner by the sink. Randy was conscious of his brown arm brushing hers, and of his height, especially noticeable when she was forced to admit that her head reached just to his shoulders. She was so aware of these things that she had trouble making intelligent or inquiring sounds as he talked about his day.

Then, without warning, he switched the focus to her. "What did the Great White Boss in New York want?"

"He just wanted to be sure I'd arrived safely."

"Micajah thought he didn't seem pleased about your aunt's wildlife shelter."

"He—was surprised."

Travis gave a hard, tight laugh. "Micajah thought it sounded as if he were trying to get you to come back—as if you had to threaten to quit to make him pull in his horns."

"If Micajah overheard, and I suppose he couldn't help it, I don't think he should have told you!" Randy flamed.

"He didn't. Not voluntarily, anyway. I dug it out of him."

Speechless for a moment, Randy glared up at Travis' blandly self-righteous face. Vainly, she searched for words scorching, blighting, and venomous enough to tell this impossible, overbearing, condescending man what she thought of him.

"How dare you!" he said obligingly, speaking for her. *"What business is it of yours! Stay out of my affairs!"*

"Ohhh!" Randy breathed, flinging down the dish towel and clenching her fists. "You—you're insufferable!"

"Sounds like Lover-Boss is a touch that way, too."

"You're not even an eavesdropper!" Randy choked, maddened by his lofty coolness. "You spy second-handed! You—"

His eyes sparked like flint striking steel. "Some things I don't do second-hand."

She tried to dodge past him but he caught her, bringing her against him so that his strong deep heartbeat seemed to thunder in her ears. Deliberately, he brought up her chin, letting his hand rest on her throat as he kissed her.

She struggled, but he was far too strong. He held her firmly, though at the back of her mind she knew that he was taking care not to hurt her.

He held the kiss, moving his mouth wooingly, insistently over hers till she thought her bones were melting, and that she would fall if he didn't hold her. She had never felt like this before, not remotely, and she was afraid to. It swept her off balance, destroying judgment, memory, everything but the closeness of him, the harsh tenderness of his lips and arms.

He was the one, finally, to move away. She leaned weakly against the cupboard, taking some satisfaction from the fact that he was trembling, too.

"Miranda—"

7

With a tremendous effort, she drew herself erect, fighting the feelings and confusions he had roused. "Is that how you prove you're a man around here?" she asked with desperate scorn. "Mauling women? Trapping them in corners?"

He took a step forward, checking himself abruptly as she shrank from him. A muscle twitched in his jaw. "Maybe I was fighting fire with fire."

"What do you mean by that?"

"If one man can talk you into painting Quality Lumber as a jolly giant, maybe another can jar you into taking a closer look."

Was that it? Had he kissed her like that just to undermine Greg and the Quality assignment? Pain stabbed through Randy, and it didn't have much to do with outraged pride or holy wrath at being manipulated.

"Don't sacrifice," she said icily. "I want to see what Quality's doing in the Thicket, and then I'm capable of making up my own mind about whether to do the account."

"Even if you won't, I bet Lover-Boss will!"

"Don't call him that, damn you! It's his agency. I can't forbid him to handle an account."

"And I suppose he'll buy your wedding ring with some of the proceeds!"

"You know a lot that's none of your concern! Did you pry that out of Micajah?"

"Miss Corinth told me."

"Oh." Randy felt betrayed, though she could understand her aunt's prejudice against anyone who might conceivably bring hardship to her beloved wild creatures. Swallowing, Randy lifted her chin and forced herself to speak calmly. "What ecological barbarity do you want to show me tomorrow? I'll look at whatever you choose, but you have to promise one thing in return."

"Not to kiss you?" he mocked. "Afraid you might get jolted out of that Madison Avenue trance you're in?"

"That's what you've got to stop!" Randy thrust. "Just stick to facts about Quality and leave me out of it."

He gazed at her. That curious melting sensation swept over her again. If he touched her then—

But he was apparently exercising some willpower of his own. "It'll be hard to leave you out of it, Miranda. But for the sake of the Thicket, I can try. I'll come by early in the morning."

They finished the dishes in silence. Travis helped move the small birds into Aunt Corinth's room and then took his leave. "Lettice's cat isn't well," he said. "She wanted to bring him over tonight so I could check him over."

As soon as he was gone, Aunt Corinth snorted. "If the cat's sick, it's from being about that female!"

Micajah shrugged. "If she can't get Travis to pay her any mind one way, she'll try another. She always gets what she wants, from the old Leffwell mansion to half the hussy benches, sword chairs, primping sofas, bustle benches, gas lights, petticoat mirrors, French court tables, fourposters, *prie-dieux*, and gewgaws in the county!" He sighed gloomily. "She'll get Travis, too, one day. She's fooled him by smiling sweet and dimpled while she flutters those eyelashes and asks his advice about everything out in the big bad world."

"She's got an adding machine instead of a heart," said Aunt Corinth, frowning. "Surely Travis can see through her?"

"He thinks she's a brave little widow woman who polishes up his antiques and brings him walnut cream cakes in return for his fixing her toaster and doctoring her and her cat."

"She polishes the furniture?" demanded Aunt Corinth.

"With a special lemon beeswax she imports from England," said Micajah. "She's particularly got her eye on that chaperone sofa Travis' great-great-grandmother brought from New Orleans when she married the first Lee in this part of Texas. Lettice has got that mahogany shining like a mirror—though so far I don't think she's managed to plunk Travis down beside her on it long enough to get across her message."

"She's a fool for antiques," said Aunt Corinth, in a voice of doom. "If she wants the Lee heirlooms, she'll be danged nigh impossible to shake loose. Drat that strumpet!"

Queer things had been happening in Randy's stomach

while her elders debated the wiles of an attractive woman whom Lee would be joining in a few minutes.

"Travis Lee's a grown man," she said tartly. "And he's certainly been suspicious enough of me! Maybe he likes this—this Lettice."

"What does he know?" frowned Aunt Corinth. "Always busy with his patients and well-baby clinics and nutrition classes! What time he has left he's messing with hurt birds or animals. Never has a chance to look for a nice girl. He's a man, and that Lettice is a tasty armful, if nothing else."

Though a ridiculous twinge shot through her at the fantasy of Travis' holding another woman as he'd held her, courting someone else with his ardently tender kisses, Randy sternly repressed the feeling.

She was engaged to Greg; her future lay with him. It was unthinkable to let Travis Lee's domineering animal magnetism undermine a comfortable, deep-rooted relationship that might lack some excitement simply because it was so natural and right.

"From what I've seen of Travis, he can defend himself," she said.

Aunt Corinth's wine-colored eyes widened, then examined Randy sharply. But Micajah had evidently decided that some music was needed. He fetched the dulcimer and sat on the bench near Aunt Corinth.

"I," said the bluebird as he flew,
"If I were a young man, I'd get two.
If one got fickle and wanted to go
I'd have a new string to my bow."

Randy smiled in spite of herself, wondering without much trepidation if Greg was noticing Sue a bit more. It had been a long day. The sweet plaintive sound of the dulcimer and Micajah's pleasantly husky voice soothed Randy; the angry pricklings subsided, and her eyes grew heavy.

Shielding a yawn, she got to her feet. "If you can manage, Aunt Corinth, I'll go to bed," she said.

Micajah winked as she and her aunt exchanged kisses. "We'll make do, Miss Randy. Sleep sweet!"

Was his long-denied suit prospering a little, or was Corinth Redwine simply making the best of a situation imposed by her temporary invalidism? Hoping that her aunt would finally drop the romantic ban, Randy said good-night.

46

The kitchen was where Travis had kissed her; he had played head-waggling with Penzance there by Aunt Corinth's bathroom; he'd paused here on the breezeway to tease her about Penelope's desire for her dusting powder puff. Already the house was full of memories, and this was only the second night.

What would it be like at the end of a month?

At the end of a month, she would go back to New York. Shortly afterwards, she would marry Greg. This would all seem like another world—distant and haunting, as elusively archaic as the songs Micajah sang to the dulcimer.

Greg was reality. He was her future. She set her mind on him, concentrating on remembering the intimate restaurants where they had dined and danced and planned enthusiastically for Summit. But Travis' lean face kept intruding.

It didn't help a bit to try to recapture the security of Greg's arms. Travis reached between them, taking over. Why, damn him, she wasn't even in charge of her dreams anymore!

After a long time, she slept.

Next morning Aunt Corinth said it was time for Woody and a few of the older woodpeckers to be moved into a large outdoor cage where they could fly freely. After a month or so, the door would be left open and they could depart as ready. When the indoor cages were cleaned, most of the bowl babies were mature enough to be switched to them, and, following her aunt's directions, Randy washed the bowls in the porch sink and left them to air on a shelf till they were needed again.

Travis had come in time to feed the outdoor birds. He treated Randy with courteous reserve, which she found infuriating, especially when she wondered if it had anything to do with the welcome he'd had from Lettice last night.

Over breakfast, Aunt Corinth approved of his taking Witchie back to the swamplands. "Wear my gardening gloves and keep hold of her bill no matter how unhappy she acts," she told Randy. "Gronker pecked you out of reflex, but Witchie would put some soul in it."

It dawned on Randy that she, of course, would have to hold the anhinga till she could be released, or drive the pickup over appalling roads. The thought of Witchie's long needle-sharp beak with its serrated edges gave Randy gooseflesh, but she couldn't admit the fear to Travis.

"You young folks get started," ordered Micajah. "I can do

the evening feed if you're late getting back, so take the day and make the most of it."

Make the most of a guided tour to disaster spots which everyone seemed to think would force her into a choice between conscience and the Quality account, which was vital to Greg and thus to her? Enjoy holding that snake-necked anhinga? At least it wouldn't be a dull outing!

"Onward!" said Travis, finishing his orange juice.

Out on the porch, he located a stout cardboard box, pulled on heavy rubberized canvas gloves, and tossed Randy a smaller pair as he selected a long-handled net. Apprehended by Gronker, who went off in a sulk when shown that the box was empty, they crossed to Witchie's pen.

She clicked excitedly when Travis opened the door. "Keep back," he warned Randy. "I'd rather tangle with an expert's knife than an anhinga's beak."

Witchie struck at the net with lightning speed. Before she could retract her long neck, Travis settled the net over her, entered the pen in a stoop, and got hold of her thrusting bill before he removed the net.

In seconds Witchie was in the box, bill still firmly restrained by Travis' gloved hand. "I'll carry her to the pickup," he said. "Will you put the net up so none of our curious friends will get tangled in it?"

Randy hung the net back on its hook, then went through the back yard gate that led to the garage, which had once been a stable.

"Fasten your seatbelt and snug on your gloves," said Travis, as Randy clambered into the pick-up. "Ready?"

Randy stared at Witchie's glittering eyes, gulped, and nodded. Travis put the box on her lap and shifted his grasp on the beak till Randy had it firmly in her fingers. "You can steady her with your other hand so she won't scoot around on the cardboard," said Travis, sliding under the wheel. "It's always a relief to release anhingas; they never get used to captivity. Cormorants can be tamed, and in the Orient they're trained to fish for their masters."

"Aunt Cornith doesn't keep pets?"

"Birds like Gronker who can't survive wild do become like pets, of course. And we'll all miss Penelope when she decides it's time she went back to the swamps."

"Penelope?" cried Randy in dismay. "I thought she would always live at the house."

"No. Your aunt found her early this spring, almost dead of

48

exposure. She took her home and tucked her in amongst hot water bottles. She's what you might call a teen-ager now. By fall, she'll probably leave us. She's already starting to visit the swamp. One day she'll just stay there."

Randy felt almost tearful. Travis seemed to guess. His austere manner thawed slightly, and he cast her a kindly glance. "Cheer up. Your robes and powder puffs will be safe at least. All right. Time for your lessons. But don't let any of the startling things I say shock you into letting go of Witchie's beak! This is a magnolia-beech community, one of eight ecosystems in the Thicket. These communities range from tall grass savanna to swamp and are caused by abundant rainfall on over a hundred different types of soil."

"But I see lots of different trees besides magnolia and beech," objected Randy.

"Sure. There's white oak, shumard oak, and swamp chestnut oak, loblolly pine, sugar maple, hickory, ash, basswood, holly, and lots of smaller trees and shrubs—yaupon, viburnum, wisteria, witch hazel, buckthorn, and so on. The Thicket is a crossroads where you can see semi-tropical palmetto palm, northern maple, southern magnolia, and even yucca of the desert."

As he talked, Randy's brain whirled, though not to the extent that she loosened her grip on the annoyed Witchie. There were about a hundred trees native to the region, over a thousand kinds of flowering plants, thirty kinds of wild orchids, a sort of gentian found nowhere else in the world, and dozens of kinds of ferns.

Travis explained that though the Thicket had once covered three and a half million acres, it had shrunk to about 300,-000, most of it cut-over trees. A bill was passed in 1974 creating a Big Thicket National Preserve of 84,550 acres, which would protect remnants of the Thicket in scattered units ranging from bayou to upland.

"It's a lot better than nothing," Travis admitted, "but the Interior Department has a year to plan the preserve and five more years to buy up the land. Meanwhile lumber companies are chewing away, and heaven only knows how much will be left by the time the preserve is finally put together."

"Why, that's wretched!" Randy breathed. "How can anyone—"

"Quality Lumber's leading the pack," Travis said.

The beech trees began to thin out, yielding to swamp chestnut oak. Cypress and hickory grew high, and azalea rioted in

49

rosy flame while ferns and toadstools colored the forest floor, spangled with wildflowers. Travis named yellow jasmine, hawthorn, rhododendron, and fragile light purple wisteria.

"We're edging the bayou, so we can let Witchie go soon," he explained. "Then we'll drive to Quality's operation, stop at my house for lunch, and meander through the bayou parts this afternoon. It's probably different from anything you've ever seen."

Randy glanced around in awed delight at giant cypresses, pale green-gray feathery Spanish moss, the way sun filtered to coffee brown waters. Birds flashed here and there, and a woodpecker, much bigger than the ones she'd helped feed, drummed away.

Travis stopped the pick-up. He came around and took the box, carefully taking control of the anhinga's beak as Randy sighed with relief and worked her cramped fingers. Travis carried the box to the edge of the sleepy water, set it down, and sprang back as he released Witchie's beak.

She struck after him but missed, gave herself a huff and puff, tipped over the box and immediately saw a limb hanging over the bayou. Climbing along this, she surveyed her regained world for a few seconds and then dived into the water. In a moment she raced past, body submerged, only her head and beak showing as she stretched them at an angle that truly made her resemble a snake.

Travis picked up the box, put his gloves and Randy's in it and tossed the carton in the back.

"Don't I get a congratulatory kiss for sending that mean-tempered bird on her way?" he asked.

"Why?" countered Randy. "You were protecting your own hide."

"Next time I'll collect before I take her out of your lap," he threatened, and jumped into the seat. "All right! Next stop is Quality Lumber's slash pine plantation, and I hope that after you've seen it, you can still enjoy your lunch."

8

One minute they were beneath a dense, many-layered roof of giant trees, magnolias heavy with creamy white bloom against dark green glossy leaves, beech and dark loblolly pine, while under these ranked what Travis named as gum, oak, maple, holly and blooming dogwood, trailing jasmine and honeysuckle, grapevines and whiskered Spanish moss. Flowers and fern carpeted the loam of decaying leaves, fallen limbs, and old trunks.

Then, with fantastic suddenness, they were in a wasteland. Withered flowers and vines, branches, and young trees lay smashed and broken, shoved into straggling piles by bulldozers that were attacking undergrowth at the other side of the vast ruin. Some of the waste stacks had been fired and smoked in a way that reminded Randy of some war-ravaged place. One machine seemed to be actually tearing at the earth, ripping it, rooting out anything alive.

"Soil-shredder," Travis said. "After big trees have been chain-sawed and hauled off, the stumps, shrubs and roots have to be cleared away before the pines are put in. So the shredder pulverizes the cleared land. Lumber companies have done this to hundreds of thousands of acres of the Thicket." He waved his arm. "Now what do you suppose happened to the nests and dens and burrows of birds and animals who lived in them?"

Randy felt sick. Fledglings like those Aunt Corinth cared for painstakingly must have perished by their hundreds. Even those escaping had lost their homes, their hunting places. It was like seeing the carnage of a battlefield where only one side had weapons.

"Now I'll show you what happens next." Travis put the pick-up in gear, and they jolted past burning stacks of what had been green, flowering, alive and beautiful.

"Is this Quality land?" Randy asked.

Travis nodded. "They bought it. Of course some of us

51

don't think that you can buy the right to destroy a whole region any more than one should be able to pollute air or water though that's done, too, by industry."

The devastation stretched for miles. Then the savaged area ran into interminable rows and rows of young trees, planted like corn in mathematical regularity.

"Slash pine," Travis said. "If beech or oak or magnolia try to grow back, herbicides will take care of that."

"It—it sounds awfully bleak." Randy stared at the geometrical rows reaching out of sight with the stripped land on one side and the great Thicket behind them. "Will birds live in there?"

"Monocultures are never good wildlife habitats. If they can survive pesticides and herbicides, and if there are enough insects to feed them, there may be some vireos, flycatchers, and warblers. Pine seeds would supply some food for birds and rodents. But there's no way for diversity to exist in such a place. It's for growing pine that has only one use: to be harvested."

"You won't deny that we need lumber?"

"You won't deny that we waste a lot of it? They talk paper shortage, but how much junk mail do you throw away each week? Anyway, trees can be cut selectively so that a forest never disappears, or loses its variety."

Randy felt like crying, and not because it would be utterly impossible to do public relations for Quality after seeing this. That was so clear, she didn't even have to think about it— one of those decisions made instantly and irrevocably at gut level. Nor was she much perturbed at Greg's probable reaction. When he understood the extent of Quality's destruction, surely he wouldn't want their account.

No, what she wanted to cry for was the forest, the shredded roots and vines and flowers, the sterile lonely regimented march of pines, the loss of wings and padded footfalls, scents and colors and changing leaves.

Travis swung the pick-up around. Randy was on the side of the old Thicket as they drove. It seemed impossible that it could vanish, but all she had to do was glance at the smoldering brush and chopped soil to her left.

She had expected Travis to preach and thunder, but he said nothing. At the beginning of the bulldozed land, he took another road leading into the deep forest, blessedly different from what he had just shown her. Birds sang again, flashing through the trees. Squirrels and rabbits darted on their errands, and the air was rich with flowers and the pungency of old leaves returning to soil.

The road ran along a clearing with a magnolia-lined drive leading to an L-shaped house of gray clapboard, weathered so that it blended with the forest beyond. Roses, ivy, and honeysuckle festooned a long veranda that stretched along the front and side of the house, and graceful rose-trunked crape myrtles graced the curve of the L.

Parking in front, Travis got a glove from the dash compartment and came around to help Randy out. "Would you like to meet Glory?" he asked, as if he knew she was too distressed to enjoy food just then.

"Your eagle? Oh, yes!"

"Glory belongs to herself and the sky, even if she's not able to get all her food by herself." Travis led the way around the house into a kind of scattered orchard where apples and plum and cherries were in bloom with bees humming from pink blooms to white. Stumps were located here and there, a few crowned with thatched shelters. There were several large cages, each holding a birdbath, perching log, and large flat stones, and Travis introduced Randy to the residents.

The dark-backed and masked bird with the white underbody was an osprey. He had been hit with buckshot but was healing and would be able to hunt again soon for his own fish. There was a red-shouldered hawk with a pin in a broken wing. Travis thought she could take to the air again, but the red-tailed hawk in the last cage made him shake his head.

"Shotgun sent over two dozen pellets into his wing and leg. He was living on roadside kills when I found him on the Muscateen road. I put an intermedullary pin in the wing, but it went on decaying. So I tried transplanting a piece of bone from a dead hawk's wing into Rufus'. Don't know if he will fly again, but I think he'll live now. He's scrappy."

"What do you do with birds that can't fly or hunt?"

Travis' gray eyes rested on the beautiful hawk with its splinted leg and ruddy tail feathers. "It depends on the bird." His voice was rough, and she knew she had touched on something painful to this unpredictable man who used his skill for birds and animals as well as people. "Predators like this are intelligent and individualistic. Some lose interest in life if they can't go free. They just stop eating and die. Others seem to have a pretty good time, and may graduate to the yard. I suppose that in the last five years I've treated well over a hundred hawks, owls, eagles, kites, and a very few ospreys. Close to a third of them die, and about half are permanent cripples."

"That's terrible," Randy murmured. He must have tremendous admiration for the birds. "Are they mostly wounded by hunters?"

"And farmers who don't seem to realize that even eagles eat more rodents that harm grain and crops than start to compare with an occasional lost chicken. Fishing and water birds are always getting caught in fish-hooks or tangled in monofilament lines or getting discarded plastic six-pack loops around their necks which catch on things and strangle them. Then there's the build up of pesticides. Rodents eat sprayed plants that concentrate DDT and such chlorinated hydrocarbons in their bodies, so that by the time an eagle eats hundreds of rabbits and mice, it may accumulate a lethal amount of the pesticide. You've heard about fish dying from the leaching of pesticides and pollutants into water. Birds who live on those fish die, too."

"It—it's all so intertwined!"

"Just so," said Travis. "Just so."

She knew he was thinking of the bulldozed, chopped-up forest. Abruptly he turned and led her past some apple trees. On a high stump perched a large bird with rich brown plumage and a sheen of gold on its neck feathers. Its legs were feathered down to the feet, giving the look of pantaloons.

"Stay here," Travis told Randy, pulling on the heavy gauntlet he had brought from the pick-up.

Approaching Glory, he made soft inviting sounds. She fluffed her feathers and answered him, set vicious-looking talons on his glove, and settled there, as if claiming him for her own.

"I can't hold her long," Travis explained. "She weighs almost fifteen pounds."

"What does she eat?" Randy asked, even from the distance of the trees a bit nervous of the large curved beak.

"Except for the osprey, who's a fish-lover, all these birds get beef, bone meal, and some sort of roughage meat with bones and fur or feathers that clean out their crops. I save all the fresh road-kills I find and any birds or small animals that didn't die of disease." He shrugged. "It's not pleasant to feed mice and frogs, but these birds must have some of that kind of food."

Slowly, he lifted the hand bearing the eagle. She gave a harsh chipping sound, then launched upwards, climbing. Her wing strokes seemed to hesitate a bit so that Randy held her breath, but Glory soared on, spiraling higher, becoming a distant speck against the dazzling sun.

"She's wonderful," Randy marveled. "Do you mean she can fly like that and still not be able to manage on her own?"

"Her timing's off just that shade that lets her prey escape often enough to mean that she'd weaken or take to raiding chicken pens. We put fresh meat on her block to be sure she stays healthy." He slipped off the thick glove. "Now let's go see what Mrs. Prosper has for lunch."

There were hot muffins moist with corn kernels, mustard greens, sliced fresh tomatoes, and golden eggs scrambled with chives and mugs of cold buttermilk, served on a blue-covered table on a screened porch facing the woods. Mrs. Prosper was a rounded pepper-and-salt lady, both as to hair and temperament, and her blue eyes dwelled questioningly on Randy.

"Corrie and I went to school together," she said. "I remember your daddy, too. Fancy him going off to Houston and then to New York, and not a Redwine left here since your aunt would nowise have a hunting man and those who don't hunt in these parts aren't men enough for her."

"I don't hunt," laughed Travis, buttering a muffin.

"You're a doctor," she said, as if that explained any and all peculiarities, and turned her attention to Randy. "Be nice if you came back to live. It's sad, the way our young folks leave to get work in the cities. Keeps on, Travis won't need to have that well-baby clinic."

"Oh, I count on being in business a while yet."

"Ain't enough to be busy. High time you had a family, Travis, or the Lees will be just like the Redwines—dwindled down to a single leaf."

"Lots of other trees in the forest," Travis said.

Mrs. Prosper tossed her formidably marcelled head. "Yes, but there's a difference in seeing saplings go and losing the Witness Tree."

"The Witness Tree?" echoed Randy.

"Thousand years old and the biggest magnolia in the world," said Mrs. Prosper, with mournful pride. "You ought to show her, Travis."

"Figured on it," he said briefly, glancing at his watch. "We've got several stops, in fact, so we'd better move along."

"Well, good gracious, you might give Miss Redwine a chance to look at the house," bridled Mrs. Prosper.

Travis sighed, then grinned and bent to hug his housekeeper as he got to his feet. "All right, Poppy, you've got ten minutes. I'll go in my office and make a few calls. If the Evans' baby's fever hasn't dropped, I should stop over there."

"That's right," said Mrs. Prosper dourly. "Take care of everyone's babies but your own!"

He dropped a kiss on her pug nose. "You're just vexed because you want a houseful of youngsters to fuss after and feed and spoil," he teased, and hurried off.

Poppy Prosper sighed angrily, muttered something, then brightened as she appraised Randy with something like growing hopefulness. "More coffee, dear, or shall we rush along?"

"I'd love to see the house but the dishes—"

"That's why I'm here," said Mrs. Prosper, rising and shooing Randy in front of her into the big old-fashioned kitchen, which had bright yellow curtains and a white and yellow tile floor. "I try to keep the place civilized, though the dear Lord knows it's been a problem with old Dr. Lee's wife dead when Travis was a mite. Travis was engaged to someone in Houston while he was in medical school, but when the old doctor died and Travis decided to practice here, his society girl couldn't give up the city."

"And I suppose young Dr. Lee wouldn't give up the Thicket?"

"More'n that to it, Miss Redwine," rebuked Mrs. Prosper. "There's always been a Lee to doctor folks hereabouts, since the eighteen thirties when this was still a part of Mexico." She waved her arm down the corridor at alternating portraits of men and women who smiled or scowled or viewed each other impassively against age-dimmed gold-and-maroon striped wallpaper. "Some Lees took to the law, one boy generally went to West Point, but first and always, one son was a doctor, a good one."

A door stood open to a pleasantly comfortable but unremarkable living room with an easy chair beside a table stacked with medical journals, television and stereo, a rocker with a mending basket near it.

"I ask you," said Mrs. Prosper rhetorically, "if a healthy good-looking young man like Travis should spend his evenings reading all that truck while I sit here sewing on buttons?"

"Doctors have to keep up with developments," Randy said.

Mrs. Prosper only snorted as she resumed her tour. "My room's next, I've lived in since my husband died thirty years ago. Doc's bedroom is opposite and his office is next to that, reaching into the L with the clinic." Opening the next door, the plump, motherly woman announced unnecessarily that this was the music room, and glowed while Randy exclaimed in wonder at the gilded harp with its swam pedestal, a grand piano, polished to gleaming, with a bowl of magnolia blooms on its closed top, a small electric organ, and several cased instruments that looked like violins.

"Travis' mother played all of these," boasted the housekeeper. "To hear her play that harp! Are you musical, Miss Redwine?"

"I love to listen but I can't play."

Randy could almost see a debit flash beside her name on the scoreboard Mrs. Prosper doubtless had rigged for unmarried young women Travis knew. "Children can inherit music from grandparents," said the buxom woman consolingly. "Now here's the library across the hall."

Randy sniffed the alluring odor of old books, leather and paper, a lingering of tobacco that must have aged into the big old leather chairs and sofa, the gold velvet draperies and snuff-colored carpet. There was a reading table with lamps, reference books and a fine relief globe showing countries that no longer existed and lacking dozens of states created since the turn of the century.

A stained-glass screen stood in front of the fireplace and crossed cavalry sabers hung over the mantel, blades nicked and worn. It was a man's room, though Randy would have loved to curl up in one of the deep-cushioned window seats and feast on the treasures here, from old gold-stamped volumes to current paperbacks Travis must have bought. A crystal bowl of honeysuckle and roses graced the magnificent table, and Randy felt touched and sorry that Mrs. Prosper had gone to so much work and preparation for a woman her adored young Doctor Lee considered a money-grubbing New York huckster.

Two bedrooms proved delightful, with great fourposter beds reached by step-stools, washstands with brass fittings and Spode china bowls, elegant chairs and settees, and impressive polished wardrobes. The dining room had a long shining table surrounded by a score of tapestry-cushioned chairs. A chandelier's multi-faceted crystal pendants caught the sunlight like

57

a thousand icicles, and the sideboard gleamed with a silver coffee service while china cupboards held delicate tea sets and several china services.

The bowl of pansies on the table looked rather forlorn in spite of their jeweled velvet faces. "Such nice parties there used to be," mourned Mrs. Prosper. "Would you believe this room hasn't been used since old doctor died? Waste and a crime, I call it!"

They crossed to the last room. As the housekeeper stood back to let Randy see an ornate carved mantel, gracefully curved sofas, marble-topped tables, and all the antique elegances of an ante-bellum Southern living room, there was peal of the doorbell and sound of someone entering confidently.

Mrs. Prosper's blue eyes swung imploringly to Randy as heels clicked in the hall and a swirl of peacock blue and chartreuse halted in the door.

9

Green eyes in a heart-shaped face went over Randy as if feeding data to a computer. Dimples showed at the corners of a mouth as ripely luscious as the curves revealed by chiffon that alternately clung and floated. It wasn't the sort of dress one just threw on to visit a neighbor. And certainly the tastefully arranged French knot was meant to call masculine attention to a shapely neck sloping to smooth shoulders.

"Dear Mrs. Prosper!" trilled the vision. "You're so busy with this big ole house to manage, and I just happened to be baking, so I dropped by with a walnut cream cake for Trav." She batted swooningly long eyelashes and smiled at Randy. "I didn't know you had company. If it's all right, I'll just run on to Trav and—"

"Miss Redwine's the doctor's guest, not mine," said the redoubtable Mrs. Prosper. "He's making some important phone calls. You may leave the cake in the kitchen, Miss Leffwell."

"Redwine?" Slim eyebrows arched as a green gaze traveled slowly over Randy's faded jeans and shirt. "You're related to Miss Cornith Redwine?"

"I'm her niece," admitted Randy, ill at ease beneath the older woman's scrutiny.

A white, very soft, faultlessly manicured hand clasped Randy's reluctant one. Her fingernails were always stubby from typewriter breaks, and several days of feeding birds had not improved them. "How nice to meet you, my dear! I'm Lettice Leffwell. My mother used to go with your father. Isn't that just fantastic? We might have been sisters!"

Mrs. Prosper made a smothered sound.

Freeing herself from a hand that had a surprisingly steely grip for all its pretty smoothness, Randy introduced herself. Lettice planted a silver cake dish in Mrs. Prosper's arms and crossed to the living room's showpiece, a sofa with a gracefully arched back that rose high in the middle, legs and wood parts scrolled with lilies, upholstery of violet-blue velvet.

Seating herself on the beautiful piece of furniture, Lettice patted the place beside her.

"Do sit down," she invited. "Let's get acquainted while Trav does his ole calling. Isn't this the most cunning chaperone sofa? They called them that because some old biddy was supposed to sit between a courting couple. Are you staying long with your aunt? Don't you find it mighty dull?"

"It's been most interesting," Randy said, aware that her voice sounded clipped and unfeminine compared to Lettice's soft drawl. "I'm spending my month's vacation."

"Oh, you're a working girl?" Lettice asked in the way she might have remarked on Randy's possession of two heads. "Well, aren't you clever! Are you some lucky man's girl Friday?"

"I do layout and research for an advertising agency."

"How thrilling!" Lettice cooed. "Goin' out to all those expense account lunches and cocktails and things! How positively appallingly dreary you must be findin' it here! Dear Trav! He just dotes on Miss Corinth. Must feel it's up to him to entertain you." She pouted charmingly and leaned forward to say in a confidential manner, "He may be tryin' to show me how independent he can be, too, just a little. We have an *understanding* but oh, my dear, these men can be so crossgrained and contrary!"

A door shut down the hall, there was a snatch of whistled tune and quick footfalls. Lettice jumped up and tiptoed, finger to her lips, to the side of the door. As Travis appeared, she stepped into his arms, put her hands behind his head, and kissed him full on the lips.

"Trav, darling!" She laughed impishly, drifting away in a fashion that suggested that she was eluding him. "Here you are keeping company with this pretty girl while I've been baking you a cake! No, no, don't try to explain, you bad boy! You'll have to do penance later!"

Gliding over to Randy, Lettice pressed her hand, touched her cheek, and whispered archly, "If it gets more than you can bear, my dear, do drop over to Leffwell House." She glided to Travis, squeezed his hand in a way that reminded Randy of the surprising strength in those white fingers. "See you soon, love. Enjoy your cake."

There was the click of heels again and the sound of the front door shutting. Randy felt dazed; Travis looked that way too. Mrs. Prosper expelled a gusty breath, staring at the silver cake plate.

"What shall we do with this one?"

"Give it to the Bryans," Travis said. "With six kids, they'll make quick work of it."

It seemed a rather unappreciative way to deal with a walnut cream cake, but Randy was foolishly glad that apparently he wasn't drooling for a piece of it. Probably his medical training and a dread of carbohydrates and cholesterol. That was cold comfort, though, when she acknowledged that Lettice was even more delectable than the cream cake, remembering the easy, confident way she had kissed Travis. She wouldn't have done that without a basis, what she'd called an "understanding."

But—if Travis was so close to Lettice, why had he kissed Randy? Whatever else one might think about him, he didn't seem the kind of man to collect scalps for the thrill of it. The only explanation she could think of was that he'd been sorry for her after Gronker's attack and the other time he'd been angry, punishing her for her connection with Quality.

Yes. That had to be it.

But his mouth, his hard arms, the way he'd held her—

Rising from the lavish sofa, Randy forced down a knot in her throat and avoided looking at Travis—it hurt too much just then. She crossed to Mrs. Prosper.

"Thank you for a delicious lunch," she said. "You've been very kind."

Mrs. Prosper put down the cake dish and caught Randy's hands. "Kind, fiddlesticks! It was a treat to have you and I hope you'll be back often." She added darkly, "*Some* come in as if they owned a place and all in it, but you've a nice sweet manner, even if you do come from up North."

Naturally a long-ensconced housekeeper would resent a prospective mistress like Lettice. Ignoring the plump woman's imploring look, Randy told her good-bye and preceded Travis out of the house.

From the pick-up, she gazed back, fixing the soft gray clapboards festooned with vines and flowers in her mind. A home place. She might never see it again. Lettice would someday oversee the gracious rooms, imprint them with what was no doubt excellent taste of its sort, yet for an hour or so, it had welcomed Randy and she loved it.

"Why so thoughtful?" Travis asked, circling past the rose-trunked crape myrtles.

She could scarcely say she was sad because she wouldn't breathe in again the rich aged mellowness of beloved books,

61

marvel at the swan-crowned harp, gaze down the rows of portraits where nearly every one held some hint of Travis.

"Your house is full of wonderful antiques," she said lamely.

The pick-up leaped at his sudden pressure on the accelerator. "You like that sort of thing?"

"Well, of course I do! Any woman would, even though it might not be the way she'd want to furnish a house."

"You were just admiring it in the abstract?" His long mouth curved sardonically, and Randy suppressed an urge to kick him.

"I had no intention of coming over with beeswax and lemon oil to shine up your loveseats," she said coldly.

"That's a relief. Poppy's going to rub holes through the wood if she keeps at it."

Miss Leffwell won't let her do that, Randy managed to keep from saying.

Constraint was heavy between them now. Randy felt hostility, an edge of distrust coming from him. This made her angry as well as depressed. Was he annoyed because she'd met Lettice? He seemed to resent praise of his antiques, even.

Impossible man! What right did he have to get huffy when he had an "understanding" with a gorgeous woman like Lettice but went around kissing other people? Let him sulk! Guilty conscience he must have, and serve him right!

No matter how she accused and condemned him in her mind, though, Randy felt miserable and—well, yes, disappointed. Facing this as they drove through the high-vaulted forest made her give herself a mental shaking and silent lecture.

She was in love with and engaged to Greg. Passing attractions to forceful strangers in strange surroundings were just that—passing. Nothing to build a life on.

The scolding made her a bit more charitable to Travis. Maybe he'd been honestly though temporarily drawn to her while knowing that his future was with Lettice. Such things did happen. One just had to keep one's head and be sensible.

Thus self-exhorted, Randy tried to ease the tension with questions about trees and plants, but Travis answered in grunts and monosyllables. Randy gave up, angrier now than at first since she *had* tried to create at least a tolerable atmosphere. She braced her feet against the floorboard, folding her arms tight, and was staring straight ahead when a flash of white and black wings and a red crest jolted her from her mood.

"What a huge woodpecker!" she cried. "But he's not as big as the one I saw the day I came, and I think the other had more white in its wings."

"More white?" Travis, too, roused from his silence, and there was no mistaking his interest. "How do you mean? Can you describe it?"

Why was he so intent? The Thicket, after all, was full of birds. Still, his eagerness affected Randy. She shut her eyes, trying to summon up that flash of color. "The bird I just saw was black on back and around the bottom edges and sides of the wings."

"It was a pileated woodpecker," Travis explained. "He's sometimes called the Lord-God bird and you can hear him drumming away at dead cypress. They're getting scarce now, but we still see them. Now what about the other one you saw?"

"I didn't get a good look. Just a flash, you know. But I could swear there was white beneath and above a black band on the under wings, and white on the back, too."

"And a red crest?"

"Oh, yes, I'm sure about that."

"Could it have been?" Travis murmured. "I just wonder!"

"What?" Randy demanded. "It was a big bird, all right, but nothing as showy as the egrets or some of the herons."

Travis slowed almost to a stop, giving her a glance of amused exasperation. "The difference is that the ivory-billed woodpecker may be extinct. Naturalists have been arguing it hot and heavy for years. Just enough reported sightings from Louisiana, Florida, and the Thicket come in to make it possible there are still a few around. Wouldn't it be something if you saw one by accident when experts have prowled from here to Georgia and not seen one?"

He sounded as if lamenting the waste of such a visitation on an outlander who hadn't even appreciated its significance. "Maybe I didn't deserve it," she said coldly. "Couldn't it have been something else?"

"Not with the crest and white wing markings as you describe them. The pileated woodpecker is about seventeen inches in wingspan compared to about twenty for the ivory-bill, but it's easy to confuse them. The real distinguishing points are the white bill of the ivory bill and its white markings. Micajah saw several when he was young and thinks he heard one a few years ago. Wait'll he hears about yours!"

"If I'd heard all this before I saw it, I'd think my eyes

63

played tricks," Randy mused. "But I'm sure my description's right."

"Maybe the Thicket was trying to tell you something."

It had told her a lot, especially the cleared part where the great trees no longer grew, but she didn't feel like sharing those feelings with him now. He pulled the pick-up over to the side of the road.

"Now we hike a while," he said.

Hiking, Randy thought, was hardly the word for what they did for the next half hour. Trailing old blazes, ax marks in the bark of trees, she followed Travis over fallen logs, dodged vines and low-hanging limbs and Spanish moss, skirted bogs, and only now and then spared a glance up at the thick green roof of beech, magnolia, and loblolly with its underceiling of gum, oak, maple, holly, and dogwood. She had to watch where she was putting her feet, but this necessary precaution brought the delight of wildflowers spangling white, blue, yellow and pink, and in damper places dozens of kinds of lacy, wispy fern.

And here were orchids in the damp swampy stretches, smaller than the florists' but infinitely more delicate and varied. Shadow witch, lace-lip spiral, crested coral, snowy, water spider, ladies tresses . . .

Travis named some of them for her, smiling at her delight, understanding without words that she didn't want to pick one but wished to marvel at their hidden secret beauty springing from the dark mud.

"Like tiny Chinese dragons with open mouths," she whispered.

"These won't bite," he laughed. "Sorry, but we'd better struggle on. I have another surprise after we've seen the Witness Tree."

How treacherous her feelings were! The wonder of the orchids had crumbled her angry resentment; it was impossible to loathe a man who clearly loved such things. Randy decided gloomily that she had to squash all romantic thoughts of him without the invigorating weapons of contempt and righteous wrath.

She clambered over an immense tree trunk, saw blue sky ahead, and in a few minutes stood beside Travis in a clearing, staring up at a huge gray stump.

Covered with woodpecker holes, it was perhaps fifty feet high, and if Randy could have stretched out across it, her head and shoulders might have overlapped. She guessed its diameter at four feet. Stripped naked, it rose in that lonely place like a reproach, an accusation.

It was a thousand years growing, the largest of its species in the world.

"Look," commanded Travis.

Crossing to the stump, he pointed to holes, some closed up with pegs. "People who didn't want the Thicket protected as a National Preserve poisoned the tree. They pumped arsenate of lead into these holes. I talked to some of the experts who came out to investigate." He gazed upward at the dead, wounded stump. "Man the Master. He can saw through in minutes a tree that took hundreds of years to grow, or destroy it like this. He can plant slash pine to grow as a har-. vested crop and kill any unauthorized plant or creature with poisons. But what will be the end of it?"

Randy put out her hand to touch the weathered trunk. How lovely it must have been, spreading glossy dark green leaves which would now be fragrant with creamy flowers.

"Who killed it?" she asked.

He shrugged. "Who knows for sure? The story made the Houston papers, and the *New Yorker* magazine even ran an article, but when the lumber companies were asked about it, the management of one outfit claimed to never even have heard of the tree. Which isn't very likely."

"But doing such a thing is so senseless!"

"If you can kill or cut outstanding specimens, there's not much left to make a park for," he said. His gray eyes pierced through her. She knew he was seeing her then as an agent of the businesses destroying his beloved wilderness. He wheeled abruptly, swinging off through the trees.

10

This time they didn't linger by the orchids; Travis moved at a pace that kept Randy breathless. She had to take three steps to match two of his long ones. They sighted the pick-up just as the stitch in her side, wrenching at each step, was about to make her beg for a rest.

Spared that disgrace, she climbed wearily into the high cab. Travis produced a Thermos jug from the back, pouring what proved to be lemonade. Nothing had ever tasted so refreshing. In his calm, understated way, Travis always seemed to have on hand whatever was most needed. Not at all like Greg, for whom Randy had to be the rememberer, bearer of medicaments, and emergency aids.

They took a rutted, sometimes invisible track to the left leading into swampier land, where cypress knees thrust up from vines and palmetto's sharp spikes while great bald cypresses climbed high and trees Travis named as willow oak and water oak grew thickly. Travis stopped, this time not pulling off the track.

"Don't want to frighten what we've come to see," he said. "It's slippery. Watch your footing."

That wasn't all she watched. A few minutes along the trail, a long supple thing dropped from a limb into brown water below.

"Lots of snakes in here," Travis said. "All of the four poisonous varieties found in the United States: coral snakes, water moccasins, copperhead, and several kinds of rattlers. And for every poison kind there must be about a half dozen harmless sorts."

"Do—do you get many victims?"

Travis stopped, looked back at her, and burst out laughing. "Only a couple in all my time here. Neither one died, and in both cases they were trying to kill the snake. Snakes are much more scared of you than you are of them."

"Impossible!" choked Randy.

66

Then, in the sudden way the Thicket had of presenting surprises, they stood on the bank of a sluggish bayou with an island some distance from shore but close enough to see birds nesting in the trees, the same birds she knew from Aunt Corinth's back yard.

Blue herons, green herons, snowy egrets, anhingas, and several fantastic birds with pink legs and wings, white necks and long bills flattened broadly at the tip. One approached another in a large stick nest; it seemed to be bowing. A faint clucking sound floated across as they traded places.

"The proud father will look after the babies now while mama fishes for a while," Travis explained. "They're roseate spoonbills. The young ones will be flying in a few weeks, and soon after that they'll start back to Mexico."

The bright or white birds against dark foliage resembled a sort of vast, widespread Christmas tree, so exquisitely beautiful it was hard to believe.

"The snowy egret has fifty-four feathers forming that gorgeous plume," said Travis. "About the turn of the century egrets were slaughtered to the verge of extinction so their aigrettes could ornament ladies' hats and boas. In nineteen-o-two, egret feathers brought thirty-two dollars an ounce—double the price of gold."

Randy shuddered to think of the lovely birds on the island being killed for vanity and greed. How could people be so cruel? Yet wasn't it as ruthless in the long run to destroy bird and animal habitats?

A white-plumed bird with dark green back and head winged by, and Travis said softly, "Did you know one Japanese emperor loved the black-crowned heron so that he gave it the rank of a court noble?"

"He looks lordly," Randy said as the bird lighted on a cypress knee. "Do you suppose Witchie came from this island?"

"If she did, she'll find her way." Travis squinted at the slanting sun. "And we'd better be finding ours."

Randy took a last sweeping look at the enchanted island, the jewel-like birds. One of life's perfect visions, so lovely that her heart turned over.

The mother spoonbill, wings glowing pink against the sun, flew in to the nest. Two snowy egrets, necks arched, seemed to be talking to each other. Randy could have lingered for hours, but Travis was already well down the road. In fact, when she turned, she couldn't see him.

Remembering the snake, Randy plunged through the swamp, suddenly a bit panicked. Her foot skidded on leaves, sliding over mud, and she tripped forward, hands and one knee taking the brunt of the fall. Her hands sank in mud up to her wrists. Better than cutting herself on stony ground, but a good deal messier. Her knee had hit a fallen limb with enough impact to tear her jeans and scrape the flesh.

Shaken, the sharp stinging pain of the skinned knee bringing involuntary tears, Randy pushed up awkwardly, hoping above all things that somehow Travis wouldn't see her like this.

He already had. He must have heard her fall for he was loping back, lifting her to her feet, looking her up and down with real concern.

"That knee!" he said. "Hurt anywhere else?"

She shook her head.

"Come along then, we can wash you off with the water I always carry in the back of the truck, and I'll douse that scrape with antiseptic."

Keeping her mucky hands outthrust, Randy didn't resist as he steered her up the track. Once at the pick-up, he opened the tailgate and lifted her up on it as easily as if she had been a child.

"Hold out your hands," he said, unscrewing the lid of a plastic jerry can.

She washed off the black gumbo as he poured. From a tin box he unearthed a scrappy, rather musty towel. She dried her hands while he rolled up her jean leg and washed her knee.

The water smarted, but it was nothing compared to the sensation of being scalded with liquid fire caused when Travis drenched the deep scratches with antiseptic poured liberally from a half-gallon bleach bottle.

Randy gasped, caught in her breath, and squeezed her hands and eyes tight to keep from crying. The stinging faded into the shock of a hard sweet mouth finding hers, the comfort of strong arms. But he raised his head almost at once, held her against him so that she heard the steady strong pound of his heart.

"Better now?" he asked, stroking her hair.

Bedside manner! Of course, as a doctor who must see lots of children he automatically dispensed sympathy along with treatment. Humiliated at the way she'd misread his actions—

thank goodness, he couldn't know!—Randy summoned a careless laugh and slid free of his protective arm.

"Fine, thanks." Why did her stupid voice stick chokily in her throat? "Now I have made us late! We'd better hurry."

"Keep that leg rolled up," he said. He helped her into the cab, closed the tailgate, and when he slid under the wheel his face was unreadable, though his jaw seemed set. It was a long way home but neither said a word.

Penelope was carrying twigs to dump in the front yard birdbath, but she abandoned her game to flash out to meet them. Travis knelt to tickle her stomach while the little otter writhed and chuckled. Randy patted her between her small neat ears and went inside, bending to kiss her aunt who had evidently just finished feeding the baby birds.

"What did you think of Goldie?" inquired Aunt Corinth, after Randy had explained her skinned knee.

"Glorious," laughed Randy. Then she sobered. "She flies so beautifully. It's hard to believe that she'd starve without supplemental feeding."

"It's a miracle she can fly at all," said Aunt Corinth. "Did Poppy Prosper give you a good lunch?"

"Delicious. She's so proud of the house, too. I could have spent a week in the library. But—"

"But?"

"Lettice Leffwell brought over a walnut cream cake. She's gorgeous. And she made it plain that she'll be mistress there one day."

"She wants to be, that's no secret." Aunt Corinth's head lifted as if to a battle cry. "But she can't make Travis marry her."

"He wasn't fighting her off." Bitterly, a vision of Lettice's ripe charms thrusting into her mind, Randy added, "What man would? Even if she couldn't polish antiques and bake walnut cream cakes?"

"Mmmf." Aunt Corinth simmered a moment, then struck the arm of her chair. "Drat if I didn't forget, child! The bottom of the refrigerator's full with a florist box all the way from Beaumont. It was all I could do to keep out of it." Her russet eyes pleaded. "Could you open it in here? I love surprises."

And probably didn't get many of them, apart from the often heartbreaking ones associated with her animal rescue work. Randy made a silent vow to send her aunt a gift from

69

time to time as she hurried to the kitchen, calling a greeting to Micajah who was shoving vitamin capsules into fish for the evening feed.

"Hey, I want to see what's in there, too!" Washing hastily, Micajah came in, hazel eyes sparkling with curiosity.

The flowers had to be from Greg. His tributes, though occasional, were always spectacular. More apprehensive than pleased, Randy dragged out a somewhat crumpled cardboard box that had preempted the bottom third of the refrigerator. "Must be a whole bouquet!" Micajah said.

Randy would have preferred not to expose the contents to Travis' eyes, but she couldn't rob Aunt Corinth of the thrill of the opening. Besides, it might be good for Travis to see that some man did value her.

She took the box into the living room, putting it down on the floor near her aunt, and removed the lid just as Travis came in.

Aunt Corinth made a murmuring sound, Micajah gasped, and Randy just stared. It was a plate-size double orchid, white with purple and gold markings, nested in fern and ribbon. Utterly magnificent and completely unwearable, even if she had been going anywhere. There was no detectable scent. In its opulent perfection, the flower seemed more a creation of man than any part of nature.

Glancing up, Randy met Travis' gray eyes, remote and almost scornful. With a pang, she remembered the wild orchids of the swamp, their rare and lovely shapes and colors.

"From your beau?" queried Aunt Corinth, leaning forward.

Randy nodded. The card said, "Forget me not—Greg."

"Must have cost a bundle," said Micajah with a soft whistle. "Just delivery from Beaumont would be a pretty penny."

"Madison Avenue's Prince Charming must not understand the social opportunities around here," drawled Travis in a blandly hateful way. He quirked an eyebrow at the immense bloom. "Even in New York, though, how would a pint-size like you wear that thing? As a sunbonnet?"

"I could wear it pinned to my waist," Randy said, with as much hauteur as she could summon.

"Wouldn't last long if you were dancing," Travis said with a maddening grin.

"You could float it in a bowl of water," suggested Aunt Corinth.

"How about a tub?" chuckled Micajah.

"There's an empty terrarium in my bedroom," said Aunt Corinth. "It would look pretty in that."

Randy nodded, ignoring Travis. Now he'd think she liked extravagant showy things. But why should she care what he thought? The men went out to feed the backyard birds while she located the terrarium, dusted it, and filled it with water.

She set it on a stand near her aunt, unwound the florist's tape and wire, and floated the horticultural triumph along with the fern. It *did* look glamorous, and Aunt Corinth regarded it with real pleasure, though she spoke with a renunciatory sigh.

"You should keep it in your room, dear. After all, it's from your young man."

"I'd rather share with you," Randy said. In truth, the only nice thing about the monster orchid was her aunt's girlish admiration for it.

She went to change her torn jeans for a skirt that wouldn't rub her knee, and started getting dinner.

Travis didn't stay for the meal but left as soon as the outdoor birds were fed, with, Randy thought, a parting curl of his lip for the huge orchid. After the dishes were done and the tiny birds tucked away for the night, Randy excused herself to write a letter to Greg. Micajah was tolerant of her company, but it was obvious that he treasured the time he got alone with his disdainful lady. Heaven knows, he earned it!

"Don't your hounds miss you?" Randy asked, on her way out of the room.

"Eh, maybe," granted Micajah a bit shamefaced.

"You can get back to them soon," Aunt Corinth said crisply. "You could take over the feeding now, couldn't you, Miranda?"

Micajah gulped. The proud old silver head turned pleadingly toward Randy. He was such a darling! Especially compared to surly, opinionated, blond-loving doctors. With scarcely a qualm at her mendacity, Randy gave a shudder of inadequacy.

"Please, Micajah, won't you help a few more days at least? I'm a little nervous of Gronker, and I couldn't feed Moses those live minnows, and I don't know how to release Penzance and—"

"Of course I'll help!" promised Micajah, glowing. He shuttered the eye Aunt Corinth couldn't see in a slow wink.

"You've caught on real well for a city girl, but I reckon it does take some getting used to."

Short of sounding like a cruel, browbeating woman who was exploiting her frightened niece, there was nothing Aunt Corinth could say, though she made a few sputtering sounds that were masked by the strum of the dulcimer.

Randy suppressed a soft chuckle as she passed through the breezeway to her room. Aunt Corinth was having trouble with her resolve to cut Micajah from her life. A little more of his attentiveness and she'd miss him sadly once he did stop coming. Let her get really used to his tenderness and singing and adoration and capability and Aunt Corinth would have to be downright crazed to keep rejecting him.

Randy's smile faded as she entered her room. She had to explain to Greg what Quality was doing in the Thicket. Say why she couldn't do copy for them, and why she hoped he'd turn down the account.

It would be a long, long letter.

It was not only long, it was also difficult. Two hours later she was still struggling to express what she had seen and how it made her feel, to convince Greg that this wasn't just another account. Greg had grown up in the city and stayed there. He couldn't really understand the Thicket, but if she could get across at least some of the shock of emerging from wildlife-filled flowering forest to acres of bulldozed waste and destruction, it ought to move him. And the barren stump of the Witness Tree. She had to make him see that.

Several times she thought about phoning, but Greg had a tendency to talk over someone, refuse to hear arguments that didn't agree with what he wanted to think. If she got it all written out, however awkwardly, he'd have to at least glimpse the issues.

He'd be on the line at once, but she'd have presented her initial case. Also the fact that she'd troubled to draw up a defense for the Thicket would carry some weight. Greg was a phone person. Written material both exasperated and intimidated him.

It was after midnight when she signed her name and collapsed into bed. Dreading a prolonged battle with Greg, taunted by the memory of Lettice so confidently at home at Travis' house, Randy could not sleep, exhausted though she was. The most disturbing thing of all was that Travis had kissed her again. Once more it must have been as consolation,

72

an instinctively sympathetic reaction, but her heart hadn't known that and her blood had raced—

Then she remembered the island rookery, the white and pink and dark birds gleaming in their low nests while Japanese heron nobility stalked the reeds. She saw again the fragile, many-colored small orchids rising from the dark swamp, Glory circling to the sun, and at last she slept.

11

There was no mail pick-up on Sunday from the box at the main road, but Micajah had to go to Muscateen and said he'd airmail Randy's letter from there. Travis had told him about her possible sighting of an ivory-bill, and Micajah wanted to know every detail.

"I'm sorry," she said at last, half laughing, half irritated. "I couldn't tell if it had a white beak. It was just a flash. If I'd known I was going to see an extinct marvel, I'd have had binoculars and a field guide at the ready!"

Micajah gave her a reluctant grin, but his eyes still gleamed with eagerness and a kind of dreaming. "I'd sure like to see one before I die. Make me feel that the Thicket would last in spite of everything. Of course with you young people movin' away—"

"*I* never lived here," Randy pointed out, and refrained from adding that it was a shame he and Aunt Corinth couldn't have buried their differences long enough to have perpetrated some Thicket-loving progeny.

Micajah seemed to read her mind. His smile grew even more rueful. "Honey, you're lucky if you find out what you want early enough to go after it. Don't add to the hassle by being too proud or too sure about everything."

Before she could answer that, he pivoted with that careless woodsman's ease that never ceased to charm her, and took himself off. Randy finished the breakfast dishes and went in to her aunt.

They fed the drumming little woodpeckers and purple martin, moved the last bowl baby into a cage, and Randy put two more nicely feathered birds out in the big flyway. She was always glad when a bird could leave the small confines for the roomy though protected outdoor pen.

Gronker, whose name she had extended to Gronker the Greedy, left off visiting with Penzance to hustle officiously about as Randy slipped the woodpeckers into their new space. She scolded him fondly but didn't pet him, her nicked hand still a memento of the slashing speed of that gold-orange bill.

Penzance croaked wistfully, and she bent to waggle her head and gronk gently. His green eyes shone and he wagged his head in response, till Gronker sidled in between them.

"What a Napoleon you are!" Randy told the cormorant, whose back feathers shaded from bronze to black with an iridescent green cast. "Very handsome, though!"

He preened, scattering herons and egrets as he rushed to barricade the porch steps. It was an old routine by now. Randy showed her empty hands. He gave a few indignant croaks, furled his wings, and resumed his almost policeman-like patrolling of his backyard kingdom.

Randy washed and rejoined her aunt, realizing that they had very seldom been alone. Micajah and Travis had filled in while she, Randy, was learning what to do, but of course that couldn't go on indefinitely—though in Micajah's case, she'd extend the aid period as long as she could.

He wanted to be there. Travis apparently didn't, for this was Sunday and he hadn't come. He wouldn't be seeing patients unless there were emergencies. It must be his "understanding" day with Lettice. Randy told herself savagely that she didn't care, that once she got back to Greg and her regular life, Travis would seem like a stranger encountered in a dream.

But if that were so, why did she feel so alive when he was near? And why did she have a sense of waiting, lacking something vital, when he was away? Much good such nonsense would do her!

"What are you scowling for, child?" Aunt Corinth's voice broke her useless ruminations. "Does that skinned knee hurt?"

"Just a little." Randy paused by the quilting frame, admiring the animals and birds and trees. "This is the most wonderful handwork I've ever seen, Aunt Corinth. If they give prizes for quilts, you'd surely win."

"Oh, there are competitions and exhibits but I don't have time to bother. Who'd take care of my birds while I was traipsing around?" Aunt Corinth picked up the embroidery hoop by her chair and worked the needle in and out, creating a smooth flowing leaf. "I'll get back to the bride quilt when these little dickenses can feed themselves. Doesn't matter when I can move easy, but I can't hop back and forth with this durned cast on." She slanted an inquisitive glance at Randy. "I want to have that quilt finished by the time you marry. Have you set a date?"

"Oh, sometime after I get back."

"You don't sound awfully enthused."

Randy forced a chuckle, glancing involuntarily toward the orchid in the terrarium. Was that how marriage would be? Imprisonment in a transparent but solid container? The image of swamp orchids, blooming wherever they would in unrestrained profusion, flashed through her mind. The florist's orchid had been pampered and cultivated and valued. But it had never existed for itself and so it had really never been alive.

"Marriage is so—final," she said. Both because she suddenly remembered and also wished to change the subject, Randy said, "I'd love to see your other quilts, Aunt Corinth. May I?"

"Well, of course, girl!" Aunt Corinth hitched herself up and got her crutches in place. "They're in the big cedar chest in my room. Come along and I'll tell you about 'em."

Then followed one of the most fascinating mornings of Randy's life, broken by time out to thrust loaded swabsticks down gaping little mouths before hurrying back to where Aunt Corinth sat in a wingback chintz chair and explained the quilts as Randy lifted them one by one from a chest scented with spicy potpourri.

The names alone were romance. Star of Bethlehem, alternate blue-and-white diamonds shaped into eight-pointed stars on a pure white field; Triple Sunflower, geometric flowers of yellow calico with appliquéd stems and leaves; the difficult Wreath of Grapes attempted only after Aunt Corinth had become an expert, grapes cut individually from varying shades of purple, and notched leaves of deep natural green with a lattice border to represent the arbor.

Aunt Corinth's fingers lingered on a beautiful quilt worked with five different kinds of wreaths, one dominant and fairly simple, the others fancifully appliquéd with flowers or ferns or geometrics.

"I made this Friendship Quilt with my three best friends," the older woman explained. "Each of us had one like it when we were finished. See, we each made a different kind of wreath, and then the blocks were put together with that plain green wreath alternating with the fancies and one in the center that isn't found anywhere else. That was—Lord help us! Forty years ago. None of us were married, though Ruth Anne was thinking hard about it and Mary used her quilt for her wedding bed."

"Do you ever see your friends?" Randy asked, afraid that she already knew the answer but sensing that her aunt needed to talk about the memories called up by the patient stitching and bright patterns.

"Ruth Anne died young and her husband moved off with the children to Beaumont. Mary moved to Dallas, married a lawyer there. Dulcie Harbinger—Taylor now—teaches school in Liberty. Not too far away, and she and her man stop by when they're visiting family, but it's not very comfortable. They think I'm a little crazy never to have married and to have gotten this interested in wild things."

There wasn't anything helpful to say. Aunt Corinth had chosen a different life than most people, and a different path was bound to have its loneliness though there would be a special zest and pride in it, too, because it had seemed important enough to choose it over the simple and expected well-trodden way.

"I'm glad you're just the way you are," Randy said, giving her aunt a quick hug. "You're better than dozens of ordinary relations, and I'm so glad you twisted my arm a little to get me to come down. If I'd known how it was—" here she indicated the quilts, Penelope, the birds and all outdoors—"I'd have come long ago, as often as I could."

Aunt Corinth colored and gave a cough, casting a weighing glance at Randy. Then she confessed, "You don't know how glad I am that you feel that way, Miranda. Fact is, as I'm sure you've guessed, Micajah and Travis would have helped till I was up and around again. But I was hungry to see you and it seemed you were never coming and I wanted to make up my mind about what to do with this place."

"This place?" Randy frowned, looking from the hearth to the roomy old-fashioned kitchen, the floor worn by generations of her family. "What do you mean, Aunt Corinth?"

"I won't live forever, child."

She seemed the sort of person who would, but of course it was unarguable fact that she wouldn't always be here. For the first time Randy considered what her aunt's passing would mean. Strangers would live in this house, the furniture and belongings cherished through the years would be scattered, and it was extremely doubtful if the next owner would keep injured egrets and herons in the yard.

Back in New York none of this would have been apparent to Randy. Now her deepest self shrank at the idea of the old home being changed. Yet what was the alternative?

As if guessing the question, Aunt Corinth sighed and tossed fiery ringlets from her face. "I hoped you might see your way to coming back here someday, Miranda, and now that I know you, I want it more than ever. But I'd made up my mind that if you had no—no feeling for the place, no interest in what happened to it, that I'd leave it to Travis."

"Travis!"

Aunt Corinth nodded, a shade defiantly. "Oh, I'd leave you what's in the bank and the old jewelry and such. But if all you'd do with this house is sell it, then I'd see it went to someone who'd care about it and who might someday have children to take it over."

And supposing those children were Lettice's, too? That prospect made Randy feel as if she'd been kicked in the stomach.

"Does Travis know about your plans?"

"First I've talked of it to anyone." Aunt Corinth took Randy's hand in her small strong ones. "Mind, dear, I'm not trying to blackmail you into making any promises or decisions. There's no hurry, so long as there's a July snowball's chance you'll find some way to use the place."

"You may outlive all of us," Randy said. "And I hope you do! Because I really don't see any chance of my coming back. Greg's a New York boy. And it would be a shame just to use the house for an occasional vacation, though I'll always come back now and then to the Thicket since I've seen it."

"You will?" Aunt Corinth's eyes probed deep. "Then you do think it's pretty here?"

"Pretty?" Randy thought of the water bird island, the orchids, the vaulting magnolias and beeches, gaunt bald cypress, banks of fern and blooming vines. "It's beautiful, fantastic! I—I love it. But it's like a fairy tale for me, Aunt Corinth, enchanted and magic but no place to live."

Her aunt gave a snort of disgust. "Magic?" she challenged. "Enchanted? Fiddledee-dee! Next thing you'll have me either a fairy godmother or wicked witch!"

"More like Sleeping Beauty," Randy couldn't help teasing. "With poor Micajah trying to get through the thorns!"

Aunt Corinth's mouth twitched at the corners, as if she were more pleased than annoyed. "All the same, dear, folks *do* live in the Thicket and make a living one way or another."

"Not people with advertising agencies."

Aunt Corinth sighed, stroking the sparkling quilt on the frame. "Yes, there's that. Travis has been like the son I never had. Guess I hoped maybe——"

"Travis," said Randy, in a crisp cool tone that belied the pain in her heart, "has an understanding with Miss Leffwell."

"Just because she makes herself free in his house, the hussy, doesn't mean she's welcome."

Remembering how Lettice had embraced him, kissed him on the mouth, Randy felt as if a wicked blade twisted in her. "It's the way she makes free, Aunt Corinth. Mrs. Prosper doesn't like her any more than you and Micajah do, but it's what Travis thinks that matters."

"He—he couldn't love that baggage!" sputtered Aunt Corinth.

Randy shrugged, her heart too sore to argue the question.

"Well, what a do!" grumbled her aunt, glaring out the window. "If Travis does marry that Leffwell wench, I don't want this house to fall to her litter!"

Randy, in spite of her scrambled, explosive feelings, had to laugh, dipping down to kiss her aunt. "See? Your only out is to stay around! Now please tell me about the rest of the quilts."

King David's Crown, Bird of Paradise, Drunkard's Path, Rose of Sharon. Randy shook out each one, draping it across the quilting frame as her aunt explained the pattern and told when it was made.

"Of course I've given away a lot more quilts than I kept," she said, caressing the Wreath of Grapes with its vivid green and varied purples against snowy white cotton. "Quilts can be a sort of history, you know. That King David's Crown has pieces from the clothes Ephesus and I had when we were children—even scraps from the boys' shirts worked in there. I remember how proud your father was of that tartan plaid shirt. Wore it till there wasn't much fit for using in a quilt. The Rose of Sharon took dress scraps collected over a good ten years." She smiled faintly. "You sew in the summer and winter, and when you're sad and when you're happy, but in the end you've made something that hangs together, something pretty and warm that will last for years and years."

Yes, Randy thought. Even if you could buy such a creation in a store, it wouldn't have in it the hours and investment of yourself that came from planning, collecting the materials, putting them together.

"It's like buying a painting," she said. "You can enjoy having it, but you can't buy the pride and achievement of having done it yourself."

Aunt Corinth nodded. "That's exactly it. And for all there's patterns, lots of a person shows in a quilt, too. Give the same scraps and colors to twenty different women and you'd get twenty different quilts. Some will make the hardest pattern to prove they're experts, others will use something quick, and another will take an easy kind that looks difficult. Some like appliqué, some don't. Some will use embroidery and lots of fine nice touches. Some suit the pattern to the material and others don't, so that the pieces pucker or pull out."

"Good grief!" laughed Randy. "It's almost philosophy!"

"With a good deal more to do with whether a body sleeps warm or cold." Aunt Corinth held up the grape quilt for inspection. "See here? The grapes are little and the leaf notches deep so the cloth has to be close-woven, the warp and weft of equal thickness so the cut edges won't fray and ravel when the pieces are turned under for sewing. No matter how fine a quilter is, she can't make this pattern without first-rate cloth of the proper kind."

The eyes of the old and young women met above the lovely handiwork. "The right pattern for the material and the patience to plan and work it out," said Aunt Corinth. "That's the main thing. It's a shame and waste to see material used in the wrong pattern. In the end, both suffer."

Randy decided to take that parable by its parabolas. "That's what I was trying to say about my living here, Aunt Corinth. Even if my material's right, my pattern isn't."

"You're young enough to scrap a pattern if you find one that suits better."

Lettice had already appropriated the only other pattern that tempted Randy. "I'm afraid my warp is thicker than my weft," Randy said, trying to joke.

"And Travis' head is thicker than either if he gets lured into marrying that toffee-throated antique hunter!" brooded Aunt Corinth. She shuddered. "Make me some sassafras tea, child? My blood gets thick as cold molasses at the notion!"

Micajah got back in time for a cup, then disappeared till

the evening feeding so it was a quiet day. Randy did a quick clean of the house, changed the bedding, and caught up the laundry. Aunt Corinth had an automatic washing machine, but drying was done on a long clothesline rigged out behind the garage.

Travis didn't come, nor did he call. It was a long, long day. Even Micajah was in an abstracted testy mood, and he took himself off without supper, saying it was time he paid more attention to his hounds.

A bit forlornly, Aunt Corinth and Randy had thick potato soup rich with cheese and onion, hot corn muffins, sliced tomatoes, and more sassafras tea.

"Men!" complained Aunt Corinth. "Pesky things hang around till you get used to 'em, and then when they're gone, you sort of miss 'em for all they track in dirt and cause commotion."

"I love Micajah's playing," Randy said.

Aunt Corinth blinked. Then a wistful, almost shy smile played at the edge of her lips. "Got a good voice for an old coot, doesn't he?" she asked. "If he'd stuck to his dulcimer— But no, he's got to be out blaring that hunter's horn and chasing things that never offered him harm!"

"I just can't imagine him shooting birds and deer," Randy said.

"Be sure he does," snapped her aunt. She mimicked a man's tone. " 'The Chances have always been hunters.' So let him go on being a Chance and the devil with him, I'm sure! Shall we work on the quilt a bit after the little birds are tucked away for the night?"

"Oh, I'd like that!" Randy cried. "Maybe I can learn enough to make a quilt myself someday. Though," she added ruefully, "most apartments don't have room for a quilting frame."

"No, or for children either, I should reckon," said Aunt Corinth.

Children? Randy had never thought about children. How would it be to have a baby in an apartment? How would it be to stay home all day with a child? If she had a baby in this old house, there'd be a swing in the big magnolia, wild and tame pets, walks in the changing woods, gathering mayhaws in spring and nuts in the fall, having a garden, a fire in the hearth on winter nights.

Or a child in Travis' house could burrow in the big old chairs in the library on rainy days and read a path around the room, pluck the harp and take lessons on the huge piano. Randy pushed that forbidden picture away but she couldn't dismiss the comparison between physical experiences, sights, sounds and smells a child would have here and those found in a city.

It was the difference between fertile soil and concrete, forest trees and pot plants, wild orchids and the florist's almost artificial product. An adult might choose the city for its business and cultural variety, but for a young child, still living through its senses, there was no question of which environment was impoverished.

Randy did the dishes thoughtfully, already anxious about the effect of her letter on Greg—he might get it tomorrow or the next day. He would think she was mentally sick if she tried to describe to him what she'd been thinking about rearing children in the city; in fact, she suspected that they were in for some disturbing talks on a number of subjects. She was glad to hang up the dishpan and escape to Aunt Corinth's company.

12

They sat up rather late at the quilting frame, for Randy had to practice first with two pieces of cloth with a layer of cotton batting in the middle. She drew the needle in and out of this with a simple running stitch, using adhesive tape on her thumb to protect it from pricks, and when she felt she had the knack of it, Aunt Corinth put her to stitching at the other end of the frame so that they wouldn't crowd each other. The quilting pattern of stylized feathers was complex looking yet easy to do, though of course it took effort to send the needle through back, front, and filling of the quilt.

"I wonder who made the first quilt?" Randy mused.

Aunt Corinth was clearly pleased to share her knowledge. "Someone in India or Persia or Egypt. The crusaders of the eleventh and twelfth centuries wore quilted garments home beneath their armor, and the idea caught on, especially after the Big Freeze."

"The what?"

"There may have been a shift in the ocean currents of warm water, but whatever the reason, Europe turned much colder in the fourteenth century. Rivers like the Rhine and Thames which had never frozen solid began to ice over and freeze winter after winter. Quilting for extra warm clothes and bedding grew popular and was used throughout Europe."

Randy made a sound of absorbed fascination, plying her needle in and out. "I suppose it varied from country to country."

"Yes. Brocades and velvets were used in Spain, and silk and damask were favored in France. Frenchwomen developed appliqué, and it was at the French court of her mother-in-law, Catherine Medici, that Mary Stuart, Queen of Scots, learned the quilting she would pursue years later while imprisoned in England by Queen Elizabeth. The Austrian court ladies of Maria Theresa made a satin quilt for Marie Antoinette that was appliquéd with doves, flowers, and cupids. The Revolutionary tribunal that condemned her to death cited the quilt, eight years in the making, as an example of her extravagance."

Randy chuckled at her own misconceptions. "I just supposed quilting was a pioneer American product."

"Settlers did bring over old patterns," nodded her aunt. "Quilting was done in most cottages and farmhouses of Great Britain and the Low Countries after the other chores were done. Each girl was supposed to have thirteen quilts when she married, and she began on these when she was very young. The thirteenth was the fanciest and started once she was betrothed."

"What if a girl never married?" Randy asked, and then bit her lip, but Aunt Corinth took no offense, merely casting her a merry twinkle.

"She probably gave them to her niece."

"Who had moved to London," supplied Randy.

"Where there was no room for a quilting frame," finished her aunt.

All next day Randy was nervous, though she knew Greg couldn't call in response to her letter earlier than evening or the next morning. Micajah brought live minnows for Moses' breakfast and helped feed the birds, but he didn't linger. Travis hadn't been heard from since Saturday, which gave Randy a forlorn sense of desertion as devastating as it was unreasonable.

"Men, drat 'em!" said Aunt Corinth again, and Randy was inclined to agree silently.

The lack of company did, however, give Aunt Corinth time to talk about previous furred and feathered boarders. At one time or another she had kept raccoons, opossums, squirrels, rabbits, skunks, armadillos, fawns, and just about every kind of bird found in the Thicket, ranging from barn owls to hummingbirds. She also explained why a broken bone could be so much more serious for a bird than a mammal.

"Their bones are hollow," she said. "Breathed air travels through them. When a bone breaks, a kind of suction drags in bacteria with every breath, so that infection is almost sure to start. When a whole wing shatters, with all those breaks—" She shook her head. "It's a pure miracle that Travis has Goldie flying again even if she can't live off her hunting." She cast Randy a shrewd glance. "You quarrel with him Saturday?"

"No." With a sharp pang, Randy remembered perching on the back of the truck while he treated her knee, giving her that kiss which meant so little to him, so much to her.

"I think seeing that monster orchid from your beau put Travis' nose out of joint," Aunt Corinth speculated.

"He probably thought it was vulgar," said Randy. "Not that I care! Him and his walnut cream cakes!"

"He's shared them with me sometimes." Aunt Corinth's eyes shut in bliss. "Sinfully rich! Absolutely scrumptious!"

"I wouldn't have expected you to care about such caloric overkill," Randy said, feeling betrayed.

"Why not? I eat, don't I? And Leffwell women, for all their witchiness, have always made the best walnut cream cakes in East Texas."

Before Randy could damn Leffwell women and their cream cakes, the phone pealed. Almost at the same instant, Penelope made the dive for the door that indicated approaching guests, but the screen was unlocked so Randy answered the phone.

"What *is* this?" Greg's voice boomed across the wire so that she held the receiver away from her. "Is auntie an ecological freak, or have you decided to do public relations for the Sierra Club? What the hell prompted a ten-page letter? In longhand yet?"

"You haven't read it," Randy said, suddenly weary. She should have known he wouldn't. Greg liked memos—short and to the point.

"I read enough! You talk about cleared land the way Florence Nightingale would describe a battlefield! My God, Randy, what's happened to your sense of proportion?"

"You might say it got kicked right out of a sound sleep." Gripping the phone tight, Randy took a long breath and struggled to keep her tone level. "If you could see the difference between a mixed forest with vines and flowers and wildlife and rows and rows of pine—"

"It's the rows of pine that pay Quality's account. It's the biggest we've got! Don't you know that?"

Travis stepped in the door just then, holding what looked like a bundle of towels with a head and long spoon-tipped bill protruding. Aunt Corinth, startled, tried to rise.

"Oil," said Travis.

"Well?" rapped Greg in Randy's ear. "Don't you know that Quality—"

"There—there's been an accident," Randy said. "I'll call you back."

Cradling the phone, she peered at the bird Travis was holding. "Bring an empty box," he said.

"And a heating pad," amended Aunt Corinth. "Gracious, Travis, where did you find the poor thing?"

As Randy scavenged up a box, heating pad, and an old flannel blanket, Travis settled the ravaged spoonbill and told how he'd found it down near Galveston where he'd gone to spend a few days with friends. Along with dozens of other water birds nesting on a Gulf island, it had been caught in a small oil spill—small compared to the 1969 Santa Barbara spill that killed 3,000 California shore birds, the San Francisco spill of '71, and the Tampa spill of '70. Of the damaged birds, only this one was still alive.

"I brought him straight here," Travis said. "He's in shock and needs to rest a while before we even try to clean him, which will take two of us."

"I've never taken care of an oiled bird," Aunt Corinth worried.

"I have, several times. I've already gotten several table-spoonsful of butter down his throat to help clean the oil out of his system. And I've got him wrapped closely enough with the flannel to prevent his preening his feathers and ingesting more oil. Now, Randy, let's put the box in the quietest room in the house, set the heating pad under it at 75°, put in a heavy water dish, and leave him alone till he's feeling better."

Randy's room was nominated as the most peaceable. The bird seemed almost lifeless as Travis placed it gently in the box she put in the darkest corner. She remembered how lovely the rose-colored birds had looked on their island, and her chest felt tight and sore.

"Does he have much chance?"

Travis shrugged. "I can tell more about it tonight. Getting oil off is a long, tedious job, but if he survives that, he's got a fair chance."

They walked through the house together. "I've got to go see a few human patients," he said. "Took a day off from the clinic, but I can't skip some house calls. You should try to get the bird to drink by dipping his bill in the water now and then. He'll need water to get the oil out of his guts."

"I'll try," Randy said. She prayed that if the spoonbill had to die it wouldn't until Travis was back.

He was barely out the door when the phone shrilled again.

"What *is* that place, a catastrophe zone?" Greg demanded. "Did your aunt break her other leg or did an alligator with pellagra wander in?"

"A roseate spoonbill got in an oil spill."

"A *what?*"

"A roseate—"

"Never mind, I wouldn't understand if you explained it." Greg sounded a bit more composed. "Is the rush over? Can you talk connectedly a few minutes?"

This conversation was one she would gladly postpone forever but that was impossible. "Go ahead." She couldn't repress a sigh. "We can't work on the bird till he gets over his shock."

"He can't be as shocked as I am," Greg retorted, but there was an edge of amusement in his voice now. "After you hung up I finished reading your letter. My poor dear love, let me make one thing clear right now. There's no way I'll cancel that Quality account."

Had she thought he might? Really, had she? Randy's stomach squeezed tight. She hadn't *thought* so, but she had *hoped*—

"There's no use in arguing, then. But you must equally accept that I won't help with the account in any way."

There was silence. She knew he was counting to ten. "Is that fair, Randy? When I let you go down there because you could get some first-hand stuff on Quality?"

"I came down here because I had two years' vacation coming."

"You know, if you were a regular copywriter, I'd fire you for refusing a project."

Randy's temper flared. "Fire me anyway if you want to!" Her voice shook, out of control now, which made her even angrier. "We both know I've worked more like a partner than an employee, but don't let that stop you! Because I won't work on accounts like Quality's for you or anybody else. Now or ever."

This time he counted twenty.

And the tight ball in Randy's stomach knotted tighter, as if all the muscles were pinched. Aunt Corinth was offering the woodpeckers food on the swabstick but she must have heard everything Randy was saying.

"Sweetheart!" Greg's voice was cajoling, full of the charm he could exert when he pleased. "You are shaken up! I didn't realize how much or I'd have been gentler. Of course I can't

87

fire you—not till our first child's on the way. You're a funny little puritan, did you know that?"

"I'd rather think I was a responsible person," Randy said, and knew she sounded dour and self-righteous.

"Okay, Responsible Person. I wish you were in my clutches right now and we'd see what we could do about that! Did you get your orchid?"

Randy shot a guilty look at the terrarium. "It's—magnificent," she said, trying to sound excited. "Perfectly immense."

"That's what I insisted on," he said gaily. "Didn't think you'd have any place to wear it down there, but I hoped it would remind you of what's waiting for you back in the big city."

"Oh, it did!" If only he knew how garish and synthetic it looked beside the orchids in the swamp. "It was sweet of you, Greg. How are things in the office? How's Sue?"

"Sue?" This time he didn't have to stop to remember who she was. "Fine. Bright girl. On her toes but can slip a funny in here and there. Which helps a long day."

In spite of feeling that Sue deserved a chance at Greg, Randy felt a jealous sting. Was he implying that Susie's good humor helped ease the strains that she, Randy, was in some part causing with her stand on Quality?

"How *is* your aunt?" he asked. "Any chance of your feeling free to come back a bit earlier? I wouldn't expect you at work till your vacation's up," he added hastily. "But if you were here I'd take you to some places where that orchid would be right at home."

On the whole, once she'd made her feelings clear, he'd been nicer than Randy could have expected. "Bribery can get you somewhere," she said. "But not this time. I'm getting to know my aunt, and that's important, Greg. She's even teaching me to quilt."

"Quilt?" he groaned.

"It's our wedding quilt," she explained.

"That sounds better," he admitted grudgingly. "But next you'll be wielding a churn and then a spinning wheel! What's happening to you, baby? I swear you sound as if you'd stepped back to Davy Crockett and the Alamo."

"I'm several hundred miles east and a bit north."

"Randy! If I could get my hands on you—" His words trailed off. "Mmmm. Well, the time will come, angel, so while you're quilting demurely away, think about when we'll be snuggling under the product!"

"Greg!"

"My sweet, that's not a start on what I'm thinking. How I've missed you! I should never have let you go without my ring, and I'm putting in on you just as soon as you're back and we can get the license!"

It was flattering to be wanted even after refusing to help with Quality. But she wished he didn't make a wedding ring sound like some kind of property label.

"I'll call soon," he said. "Take care, love. If you dream, dream of me."

He hung up before Randy could tell him that either because of the country air or weariness, she was sleeping so heavily she didn't dream at all, not to remember.

"Started off with cannons and ended with violins," grinned Aunt Corinth. "You did right, not to let him buffalo you out of what you believe. Start giving in on things like that for someone you love, and soon what you have to love with washes away, too."

The last thing Randy felt up to was a lecture on love or cross-questioning about Greg. "I'll go see if the spoonbill's drinking yet," she said.

"He looked too done-in to peck at you," considered Aunt Corinth. "But it might be a good idea to wear a rubber glove if you need to put his bill in the water."

Randy pulled on one of the several pairs of gloves that hung from clothespins on the back porch, then went through the breezeway to her room. The bird's bald greenish-topped head rested against the side of the box and some folds of flannel Travis had arranged. As far as Randy could tell it hadn't stirred, and its coral eyes, though open, seemed not to register anything.

With great care she brought the strange long bill with its broad end forward and dipped it in the water bowl. She might as well have been holding a stick. She hoped Travis' house calls wouldn't take too long so he could get back to this exotic patient.

Releasing the bill, she reported back to her aunt. "He at least doesn't seem any worse but he wouldn't drink."

"You can try again in a while," Aunt Corinth said. "But he'll have to make an effort—he has to want to live or he won't. Comical heads they've got, sort of like a turkey's except for the beak and wattles. All that beautiful rose and white plumage topped by a clown face. They look stupid, but Travis says they're not." Aunt Corinth sighed and glanced at the clock. "Is Micajah coming to help with the feeding?"

"He said he would but I'd better go start stuffing vitamins into the fish. Shall we just have scrambled eggs and salad for supper?"

"Quick and good," approved Aunt Corinth. "And I would reckon we're in for quite an ordeal with that spoonbill, so better rest a bit if you can."

Micajah appeared with minnows for the little green heron who was now wandering in and out of his cage. Randy told the old hunter about the spoonbill and he went back for a look.

"Got him to take a drink," he said when he returned, washed his hands and helped finish preparing the fish. "Poor critter acts like shellshocked buddies I had in World War II. But if he drinks that'll help flush the oil out of his innards."

Gronker claimed his tribute as usual before allowing the mortals to dole out the other rations. Micajah paused at the woodpeckers' big flyway cage.

"See you're feedin' peanut butter and putting chopped apples and raisins in their feed mix," he observed. "Haven't lost a one of this bunch and in two-three more weeks, they can take off for good."

"I'll miss them," Randy said. "Especially Woody. He's the first bird I ever fed, and look at him now!" For Woody was growing into a handsome specimen of a downy woodpecker, and it was hard to believe he had been eating from a swab stick only five days ago.

"Sure, you get fond of wildlings," said Micajah. "When Penelope goes off for good, Corrie's going to shed some tears. But you take care of these things so they can go where they belong and live free. When a creature can't live the way it should, there's sadness in it."

As they were washing up, Randy said rather pertly, "I hope you won't rush off tonight, Micajah. Travis says it's an awful job to get oil off a bird."

"Reckon it will be. I'll go feed my hounds and come back later." His hazel eyes delved into Randy's. "Corrie glad to have me out from underfoot?"

"So you are doing it on purpose!" Randy accused.

"She's noticed?" he asked eagerly.

"Of course she has! She—I mean, my goodness, Micajah! I never thought you'd be sneaky!"

"All fair in love and war," he chortled. "And this is some of both!"

"Playing the dulcimer! Singing 'Darlin' Corrie' in that wheedling way you have! Honestly, Micajah! I ought to tell Aunt Corinth what you're up to!"

"But you won't," he said, with such droll assurance that Randy's glare turned into a chuckle. They gave each other a hug and went inside together.

13

Travis and Micajah turned up at the same time, after the small birds were put away for the night and Randy had insisted she was *not* too tired to work at the quilt. She had twice coaxed the spoonbill to drink and thought he seemed less glazed of eye and a bit more aware.

Resisting the obvious name of Spoony, she had hesitated over Valentine and then decided to dub him Valentino. But after Travis looked over his patient and declared it time to tackle the cleaning, there was no chance for frivolous thoughts.

Travis suggested the kitchen because of the mess, but Aunt Corinth insisted on being able to watch so that she could do it next time it was required. Randy, following Travis' directions, spread newspapers and fetched a pile of rags and old towels while Micajah got cornmeal and salad oil and shut the door and windows against drafts.

When Travis brought the bird in, he told Randy to put on gloves and hold Valentino's head and bill while the dirty flannels were unwound and stuffed in a paper bag.

"There are three of us so we can spell off," he said, settling on the floor. "Can you hold his bill and head, Miranda? He doesn't act very belligerent, but it's best to keep him quiet. He could die from sheer nerves and stress. We've got to be as careful and easy as we can."

He worked salad oil gently into the stained feathers, then wiped it off with rags, pressing firmly to get off the excess before he dusted Valentino with cornmeal. More rags took off the blackened cornmeal. Salad oil again, then careful blotting. Cornmeal, wiping.

After an hour of this there was a pile of greasy rags, a somewhat cleaner spoonbill and Randy was feeling the strain.

"Micajah, will you fill the tub with clean warm water and we'll give him a rinse before we go back to this," decided Travis, shrugging his shoulders up and down to rest them, though he put on more oil and cornmeal, swabbing patiently till Micajah proclaimed the tub ready.

The rinse left a scum of cornmeal and oil in the water. Travis toweled Valentino and held the spoonbill's head while Micajah took over with the cleaning. Randy scrubbed out her aunt's tub, disinfected it, made hot tea, and drank hers before taking over from Travis, who had his tea and relieved Micajah who had his turn at relaxing.

Three hours later, they were still at it. The feathers were growing rosier and whiter in the appropriate places, and Valentino had drunk more water. Randy had taken several turns at wiping, using great care not to rub the wrong way.

"Wouldn't turpentine be faster?" Micajah grunted as they started a new pile of rags.

"It'd kill him," said Travis grimly. "So would kerosene or gasoline, and detergents take out the natural feather oils and may start a breakdown of the microstructure. This and the molecular bonding make a feather repel water, and if the natural oil goes, the frizzies set in—which means the feathers will soak up water."

"You mean a bird would sink?" inquired Micajah.

"You bet. And chill, too. A lot of 'rescued' water birds die shortly after release because their feathers are damaged. They can fly before they may be able to float very long."

At the end of another hour, they gave the bird a final rinse, blotted him with towels, and finished drying with Aunt Corinth's hair dryer nozzle on a warm setting. Then Travis wrapped him in more of the old flannel blanket and put him back in his heated box.

"Doesn't he need food?" Randy asked.

"We'll try early in the morning," Travis said. "I'll be over by six, but if he has trouble and you get worried, call me anytime."

It was after midnight. Randy was stumbling with weariness. She was oily, cornmealy, and still had to clean her aunt's tub and have a shower. But as Travis' gray eyes touched her and a faint smile curved his mouth, she felt happy. It was as if they'd fought hard in a battle they might win; they could trust each other not to quit.

When she finally fell into bed that night after getting Valentino to take a drink, she didn't dream of anyone, but it was Travis she was thinking of as she sank blissfully into sleep.

She came slowly awake to a tapping on her door, fumbled into a robe, and opened to Travis, who looked disgustingly alert. At least alert enough to chuckle as he scanned her sleepy disarray.

"Wash your face," he advised, moving past her to the box in the corner, but she overtook him to look down at the bird who watched them with an ineffably mild expression. He had sipped more water, and all in all looked as if he had chosen to return to life.

Travis nodded. "Good boy. We'll see how you do with a smelt. Miranda, while I clean him up and check him, could you put a Vitamin B-1 capsule in a smelt and bring it here? And a big pair of rubber gloves, please."

Randy had been so worried about Valentino's lack of food that she gladly postponed even brushing her hair to hurry and fix his breakfast. Micajah was getting the yard birds' fish ready, and Randy told him that Valentino had survived the night and looked better.

When she returned with the fish, Travis had removed the flannel and nested Valentino in several thicknesses of newspaper. Travis offered the smelt but Valentino's coral eyes watched it without interest. Travis sighed.

"He may have to be fed for a few days. This is how—and do remember to take it easy." Slipping a rubber glove on his right hand, he opened Valentino's bill and slipped the fish down his throat, supporting his head and neck as he cautiously shut Valentino's bill and smoothed his throat with light, firm downward strokes. "He should get the idea in a day or two and feed from the hand or dish," said Travis. "Now let's put some baby oil on his feet so they won't crack and just leave him to be quiet and dry. I'll stop by this evening, but if he seems to have any new trouble, call me."

"Won't you have breakfast?"

"Thanks but Poppy's making waffles. Thinks I'm getting skinny." As she walked with him through the breezeway and house, he glanced at the floating orchid. "So you found a place to put it? I reckon that compared to it, the orchids I showed you Saturday look like they're suffering from malnutrition."

"They are smaller."

Stung by his sarcasm, Randy was not about to admit her true feelings about Greg's offering—or was demonstration more the word? An orchid like that wasn't a gift. It was a declaration.

94

Travis' mouth hardened and his eyes were freezing as a stormy winter sky. Turning his back to her, he began reporting to Aunt Corinth on Valentino's progress. Randy went out on the porch, saw Micajah was almost through feeding the big birds, and busied herself with mixing the older woodpeckers' food. She put this in the big cage along with some peanut butter, laughing as Woody and his friends stopped their miniature drumming on perches and limbs and flew to their feast.

"Moses was gone when I came this morning," Micajah said, joining her at the back door. "But he turned up about the time I was thinking about giving his minnows to Penzance." He glanced a bit regretfully from the little green heron to the green-eyed orange-billed cormorant. "They'll both be leaving soon, I'm thinking. Funny how you get attached to birds once you know 'em. They've got characters, just like people."

"They certainly do." Randy looked at the healing scar where Gronker had bitten her. "I was scared to death of Witchie. And I'll never pet Gronker again, though I've gotten fond of the arrogant little dictator. But Penzance is a darling. And though that silly beak on that gorgeous body makes him sort of a joke, I think I'm going to like Valentino."

"Spoonbills sure look feeble-minded," said Micajah. "Travis claims they're smarter than herons, but I don't believe it." He declined her offer of breakfast, though he promised to look in around noon in case she had trouble with Valentino, so once again Randy and her aunt breakfasted alone.

While she was tidying up, Randy found Aunt Corinth studying herself in the bathroom mirror. "My hair sticks out like a wire brush," she complained. "And I'd never noticed all those cotton-pickin' wrinkles! I wonder if—" She stopped, shrugged, and said defiantly, "Micajah, once he got close to me again after all these years, may have decided I'm an old fright."

"I'm sure he hasn't!"

"How can you be sure?" Aunt Corinth frowned. "The woods are full of widow women, and if he'd courted one before, I could have understood it. But I do think it was varminty of him to hang around all hours strumming that dulcimer if he's been keeping company somewhere else!"

Randy hated to see her aunt distressed, but she felt tipping Micajah's strategy at this time might deepen Aunt Corinth's mulishness and end for good their chance of getting together.

So she said with great sympathy and concern, "I have no idea what Micajah's doing, but I gather he was barred from this house for a cold eternity and it'd be no wonder if he'd made some other—friends. He's a very handsome, appealing man. If he were twenty years younger, I'd flirt with him myself."

"Oh, would you now?" Aunt Corinth's eyes shot amber sparks, and then she laughed. "Well, if Travis Lee were twenty years older, neither you nor that silly Lettice would have a chance, I'd move in on him so fast! I'm sure your New York beau is all very well but I've seen some grand men in my time, and Travis is head and shoulders above 'em."

"He's tall," Randy conceded.

Aunt Corinth gave her a reproachful look and Randy changed the subject. "Why don't I wash your hair? It must be awkward for you with that cast."

"That'd be heavenly," Aunt Corinth sighed.

So with a spray attached to the kitchen faucets, Randy washed the only faintly silvered fiery locks, toweled them, and set them on large curlers. Then she helped her aunt take a stroll on crutches around the back yard, visiting with Gronker and Penzance in particular, and finishing with a peek at Valentino.

"He kept down his breakfast," Randy noted gladly. "And he's drinking by himself. I guess I'll try him on another smelt."

"Funny creature," marveled Aunt Corinth. "But he sure looks a sight different than he did yesterday.",

"He should." Randy grimaced, moving her shoulders which still ached from the long strain of working on the bird. She heard a distant thumping. "Someone at the door?"

"Sounds like it." Aunt Corinth's hands flew to her curlers. "Can you answer it, child? I'll turn the drier on for a few minutes and be right out."

Randy opened the doors for her and then sped through the house to the front. A large blond man with a ruddy complexion and china-blue eyes stood at the screen, stopped in mid-knock at Randy's appearance. A slow, surprised smile spread across his face.

"Miss Redwine?"

"Yes, but so's my aunt, and she's the one you probably want to see. She'll be right out."

"Miss Corinth Redwine?"

"My aunt," Randy confirmed.

Should she ask him in? In the city she wouldn't have, but it

96

was different here. As if he sensed her quandary, the stranger's smile grew even broader and more reassuring.

"I'm Brock Maynard. And if you're Miranda Redwine, I'm looking for you, too, in a way. I was talking to your fiancé, Greg Hathaway, just yesterday."

"In New York?"

"Yes. My company's interested in acquiring land around here, and Greg mentioned that your aunt owned property. He also said he'd be glad when your visit was over." The big man's eyes danced. "I can see why!"

Randy colored, not so much at his words but at his frank admiration. "Come in," she said, opening the door. "I don't think Aunt Corinth will want to sell, but of course that's her decision. Please sit down. Would you like—" She started to say "coffee," but some freak impulse made her substitute "—some sassafras tea?"

"Why not?" he asked imperturbably, glancing around. "Say, this is a time trip! Old fireplace, braided rugs, and that quilt!" He crossed to stare down at it as Aunt Corinth swung through the door on her crutches, her hair attractively fluffed and shining.

Randy introduced them and went to make the tea. While the bark was steeping she fought her squeamishness and slipped a smelt down Valentino's throat, stroking it to ease its passage.

"You're doing fine," she told him. "Be a while before all that gunk fades off your pretty feathers. Your legs and feet are rosy red again. In fact, you're mighty handsome except for that face, but as long as you look good to spoonbill ladies, I guess you don't care what we think."

She washed her hands and poured pungent tea into three cups which she carried into the living room. Brock Maynard accepted his cup without noticeable apprehension and tilted her a bland smile.

"Haven't had any of this since my grandmother used to dose us with it every spring to thin our blood," he reminisced. "Makes me feel back home and then some!"

"Brock grew up on Little Pine Island Bayou not so far from here," Aunt Corinth beamed. "One of my second cousins married his uncle."

"That makes Miss Corinth and me kissing cousins," Brock grinned. "Wonder if I could stretch the kinship to you, Miss Miranda?"

Randy ignored that, feeling somewhat duped. "I—I thought—you said you were from New York!"

"I am now, but I'm Quality's contact man down here since I know the region."

"Quality Lumber?" Randy echoed, pulses starting to throb. "Quality sent you to—to—" She broke off in dismayed anger as Aunt Corinth touched her arm.

"Don't be hasty, dear," she said tranquilly. "Brock has an interesting offer. I think you should hear it."

14

Randy glanced from her aunt to Brock Maynard in stunned disbelief. "Aunt Corinth! You wouldn't sell to anyone, would you, much less Quality?"

Aunt Corinth sighed. "You don't seem to want the place, child. Don't think I told you, but I own three sections. That's 1,920 acres. Brock has offered a real good price." She nodded meditatively. "I could buy a house close to town and begin a wildlife refuge with paid people to carry on as I get too old. Set up a foundation."

Randy's head whirled. "But the company would tear down this house!" she cried. "They'd cut down all the trees—tear out the stumps, shred the ground! You wouldn't let them do that!"

"Now, now," interrupted Brock, blue eyes widening and getting even ruddier of face. "We're not vandals, Miss Miranda. Quality employs excellent management people to advise on environmental impact. You have to remember that pulp wood is a crop, just like cotton."

"Trees aren't like a short-term plant anymore than an eagle that lives twenty years is like an insect that lives a week!"

"If we can just not get emotional," coaxed Maynard.

Whirling from him to her aunt, Randy said imploringly, "I—I thought you were going to leave the place to Travis Lee since I can't come back to live on it."

"Brock is talking about a lot of money. Sounds worlds different than when I was thinking about just the house, sentimental like." Aunt Corinth's tone was brisk. "I wish you were happier about it, my dear, but under all the circumstances I'll certainly have to think on it. I surely will."

Brock frowned slightly. "The offer's extremely generous, ma'am."

"I'm not trying to run you up," Aunt Corinth said genially. "But it's a big decision. I want to discuss it with my niece and have a while to think."

The big man sipped his tea as if trying to penetrate a devious maze. "Well, Miss Corinth, if you have any questions or suggestions, please call me at the Angle Inn. I'm combining a little pleasure with business while I'm here, getting in some fishing." Rising, he nodded to them both. "If I don't hear from you first, ma'am, shall I call you tomorrow?"

"Day after," Aunt Corinth said.

Maynard looked as if he longed to say something which he suppressed, though he slanted a challenging smile at Randy. "All right, Miss Corinth. I think my company's offer will probably hold good."

"I expect so," she said drily.

He turned to the door as Micajah came whistling up. Aunt Corinth introduced them, or rather refreshed memories, for Brock clasped the old hunter's hand enthusiastically.

"My father and grandfather always said there were no hunters like the Chances and no hounds like theirs. Any chance of our getting out after a coon or something?"

Micajah seemed more embarrassed than pleased at Brock's admiration. "I'm helping out around here while Miss Corinth's laid up," he evaded.

"But you must take your hounds out some." Maynard's eyes sparkled. "I'd purely love to hear a horn again, and hounds belling."

"The Jamison brothers over at their fishing camp on Pine Island Bayou, they'll take you out," said Micajah.

"I'd sure rather go with you."

"That's mighty flattering," said Micajah, plainly distressed at seeming unobliging yet for some reason quite determined. "Just can't fit it in right now, Maynard."

Brock looked disappointed as a boy whose new kite string had broken leaving him to watch his treasure float beyond reach, but he managed to shrug good-naturedly and shake hands. "Maybe next time. My company's trying to buy all the land it can get outside the projected National Preserve, so I imagine I'll be down here pretty often during the next year or so. Your land lies in the Preserve, doesn't it, Mr. Chance?"

"Yep," said Micajah. His hazel eyes had grown cold when he heard Brock was buying land for a company. " 'Cept for a few acres my house sets on, and I'm keeping that." Bewilderment grew on his face, changing to consternation. "Corrie! You'd never be selling out!"

"I'll be moving on," interposed Brock. "If I don't hear

100

from you, Miss Redwine, I'll be in touch day after tomorrow."

The screen reverberated behind him.

Micajah seemed not to hear. He hunkered down by Aunt Corinth's chair, taking her hands compellingly in his. "Now, Corinth Redwine, what's that young pup doing here?"

"Quit smashing my fingers!" she snapped. "I don't want them in a cast, too!"

He apologized, released her sheepishly and pulled up a bench. "I want an answer, Corrie."

"Can't remember naming you my keeper," she thrust, eyes glinting as she rubbed her fingers. "However, there's no reason to keep it dark since I'm going to do what seems best to me, no matter what my interfering neighbors have to say! Brock Maynard works for Quality Lumber, and since he knows this country, they've sent him down to make offers for land that looks good to them."

"Won't look good once they clear-cut it and bring in the bulldozers," Micajah growled. He shook his head, dazed and unbelieving. "You've got to be funning, Corrie, even pretending to dream of such a thing! That's it, isn't it? You're pulling a joke on us all!"

"I'm not. I'm seriously studying over a serious proposition."

"Serious!" hooted Micajah, regaining his balance. "Cut the foolishness! You'd never leave this house, not while you breathe."

"But I won't always breathe," pointed out Aunt Corinth. "And if the place is going to strangers after I'm dead, why shouldn't I sell it now and do something useful with the money?"

Micajah groaned, turning to Randy. "Can't you talk sense to her, girl?"

Feeling helpless and rather blackmailed, Randy said, "It's up to Aunt Corinth."

"No," said her aunt positively. "It's your decision, too. If you said you'd even think of coming here to live one day, I'd tell Brock to go spit in the wind."

Randy shook her head. "I hate to think of you selling, especially to Quality. But I can't make a promise I'm not sure I can keep."

Aunt Corinth sighed. She looked suddenly very tired. "Well, well," she murmured. "I'll just have to mull it over then."

"Wait'll Travis hears about this!" predicted Micajah. "He'll think you're in a raving fever, Corrie. And I hope he'll have something in that black bag to bring you to your senses!"

She tilted her nose at him. "Travis won't like the Quality part, but when he hears I'd start a real wildlife treatment center with the money, he'll see that as a plus. Anyhow, Micajah Chance, it's my land and my life and my house! I'll do with them as I see fit!"

"You're so pig-headed it's a marvel you haven't been shot for a razorback!" glared her angry suitor.

"Yes, you'd think of something like that!" flashed Aunt Corinth. "Since you're so crazy to hunt, why didn't you take Brock Maynard out? He'd appreciate your gunning away!"

The light of battle flared in both russet and hazel eyes. Randy's elders had forgotten all about her. Expressing their anger might drag out softer feelings, too, Randy hoped. If, after all these years, something would jar them into kissing and making up, wouldn't it be wonderful? Right now, most importantly, it might put an end to Aunt Corinth's thought of selling her land.

Randy soft-toed out, but her hopes for a reconciliation were quickly blighted when Micajah joined her, pretending great interest in the salad she was making.

"How's old Spoony?" he asked. "Get another fish down him?"

Randy nodded. "Have a look at him and stay for lunch," she said.

"Thanks kindly, but I'll squint at the bird and amble along." His jaw set grimly. "I don't know what's got into Corrie but I sure don't like it. If I stay around, we'll have a battle royal."

"What's wrong with that?" inquired Randy. "You're both pretty tough-tempered people, you can handle what you dish out."

Micajah scowled. "We can live through each other's rawhiding, if that's what you mean. But I don't want to get Corrie more riled than she is. I've known her a long time, honey. She's so stubborn she won't only cut off her nose to spite her face, she'd lop off her head." He shook his head. "That's what it amounts to, sellin' this old home place! She'd be sick sorry the minute she'd signed. But if I make her mad, she might do it just to prove she can."

The way she wouldn't marry you.

Randy couldn't protest. He had known her aunt since they

102

were young together. In spite of their perverse estrangement, he doubtless understood her better than anybody else. What a waste of faithful loving! And just when his strategy of leaving her desirous of his company seemed to be working, they had to get into a broil over Brock Maynard's offer.

Brock Maynard.

Randy stopped shredding lettuce, pondered with mounting suspicion. Had Brock's conversation with Greg had anything to do with this sudden offer? If Quality was buying in the area, the proposition would have been made before too long, no doubt, but had Greg done a little nudging?

Lunch was already late. Randy quelled the impulse to rush straight in and phone Greg. The question would keep, and she'd be in better control if she thought about it first. At the same time she felt uncomfortable at needing to review facts as if she were mounting a court case rather than simply asking a question.

She asked it straight away, after lunch was over and the dishes done. She had chewed on the connection till her nerves were screaming tight, but the only explanation she could come up with was that Greg might hope her opposition to the Quality account would lessen or vanish if her aunt left the area so that Randy would have no personal stake in the Thicket.

And if he believed that—

Catching her breath, Randy dialed direct to the line Sue was instructed never to answer. When Greg came on, she said at once, "Greg, did you tell Brock Maynard my aunt owns land in the Thicket?"

"Baby!" he said. His tone deepened in gratified warmth. "I was just thinking about you! Decided to come home?"

"No," she said flatly. "Greg, what did you say to Maynard?"

"So I said your aunt owned property there. What's wrong with that? Turns out he even remembered her family name."

"You didn't just happen to suggest he start his land-buying trip with her?"

"Now why would I do a thing like that?" She could almost picture his dark brows quirking.

"Maybe you think I won't care what happens to the Thicket if my family stops living here."

"Angel! Why are you set on making such a big thing of all this?"

"Because it is big! Now that I've seen the Thicket, seen what Quality does, I'd still care about the place even if Aunt Corinth went to the moon! It—it's got nothing to do with who owns the land."

"Good Lord, darling! Are you going to start saying earth's sacred, our mother, etcetera? Don't! I've been working on commercials and my head hurts."

His weary, elaborately patient tone triggered something in Randy. "All right, I won't!" she said, and hung up, so angry she was trembling.

They couldn't talk now. If they tried, Randy knew she'd say searing, unreasonable things, and Greg would either react violently or in the patronizing manner she hated.

The phone rang. She let it.

"What was that all about?" asked her aunt. "My gracious, child, have you quarreled with your beau? You're shaking like a leaf!"

"I wanted to know if he'd pushed Maynard a little. He didn't deny it. So that means he did."

"Not a crime, is it?" asked Aunt Corinth with a lift of reddish eyebrows.

"I feel as if it were!"

Aunt Corinth shook her head. "I can't figure you, dear. If you won't take over the place, why should you care what happens to it?"

"And that's the kind of talk I can't understand," Randy said, rather wildly. "Why can't I care about something even if it's not mine? I won't be living here, Aunt Corinth, but I do love this house and the Thicket. If I can't stand to think of it being cleared off and planted to slash pine, how can you possibly bear it?"

"I don't like the idea, Miranda. But if it's not staying in the family, maybe I should just take the money and build a first-rate wildlife hospital. You've got to admit that's worth doing."

"Yes, but—"

"I have to think about it," Aunt Corinth said.

She looked so tired that Randy's conscience reproached her. Contritely, she went over to drop to her knees by her aunt's chair, taking a weathered but fragile hand in hers.

"I'm sorry, Aunt Corinth. You have to do what you think best. I—I wish I could be more help."

They sat in silence for a while, the older woman stroking the younger one's head, till Penelope bombed in, eager for attention, and Randy left her aunt tickling the otter's stomach while she went to check on Valentino.

Greg, back in New York, must be seething, but Randy, who came to a rapid boil every time she recalled their talk, found she didn't care about that. If he didn't want a scorching, he'd better just leave her alone for a couple of days!

15

Travis came by that evening and nodded his head approvingly at Valentino's progress. He and Randy oiled the bird's coral-red feet, changed the paper padding, and Micajah, in from caring for the yard birds, presented the spoonbill with a fish, which this time didn't have to be pushed down the long white throat.

"Won't he get bored, just sitting like that in the box?" Randy asked.

"He's been, and still is, under great stress," Travis explained. "Birds can die of that, even when nothing else is wrong. His preening glands are out of whack because of the oil and then the cleaning. When he begins acting restless, it'll be time to try him on some water and see if he can float. It may take weeks for the natural oil to waterproof his feathers again."

Randy stared. "You mean he'd drown if he were set loose too early?"

"That's just what I mean. Happens pitifully often. Kind folk save a damaged bird, spend hours cleaning it, feed it up, and when it can swim at all, assume it's okay to set it free. I hate to think how many 'rescued' water birds die of drowning or chilling because they're put out before their feathers can sustain them for long stretches on the water."

Randy shook her head. "It's awesome, what most of us don't know about birds and animals. They're so much more delicate and sensitive than I'd ever have dreamed!"

"They're the earth's secret heartbeat," Travis said. "I don't think we can stifle it without in some degree killing ourselves."

Leaving Valentino snug and warm, they started through the house. "Have you told him?" Micajah demanded. "Told him about that Maynard guy? Maybe Travis can talk some sense into Corrie!"

106

Travis checked, looking from one to the other. "What's this all about?"

"I thought Aunt Corinth should tell you," Randy said, sighing reproachfully at Micajah.

"Let's have a preview," Travis urged.

Pausing on the breezeway, Randy briefly explained, accompanied by profane asides from Micajah.

Travis looked absolutely stunned. Shoving back his thick unruly hair, he turned a freezing gray stare on Randy. "Did you set her up for this?"

Randy blinked. Why, the hateful, conclusion-jumping, prejudiced bigot! When she tried to speak, a lump rose in her throat, choking her.

"Think what you want!" she blazed. "You will anyway!"

She started off as Micajah admonished, "Aw, Travis! You've got it wrong. She—"

"She can speak for herself," Travis cut in. He took a long stride, catching Randy's arm. "Go along to Miss Corinth, Micajah."

The old man hesitated a moment, shrugged, and went on.

Knowing it was useless to struggle, Randy glared at her captor, who seemed to make an effort now to speak with judicious calm. "All right. Tell me about it."

Close to tears, she shook her head fiercely.

He sighed. "We can stay here all night, you know." His voice deepened as it grew almost teasing. "I'm getting tired, though. If you don't speak up, I'll just sit down and sort of use your shoulder for a pillow."

How could he be nastily suspicious and accusing one minute and then switch to winsome plaintiveness? Randy's knees weakened at his closeness; his hand sent warmth surging treacherously through her.

Denying this, hardening her spirit toward him, Randy said bitterly, "What's the use, trying to explain? You want to think the worst of me! So go right ahead. Enjoy it!"

In spite of her resolve to be like stone to him, tears stung at the corners of her eyes. She tried to pull away but he drew her close, lowering her head, taking her mouth with his. She pushed at him for a moment but the sweet, tremulous melting that had been spreading through her since his manner gentled completely swept her defenses away. She gave herself wholly into his arms, letting her hands stray up to caress the back of his neck.

Strangely, she felt more cherished and protected in this difficult, irascible man's arms than she ever had with Greg. But—Travis had that "understanding" with Lettice. This couldn't be, for him, anything but an impulse.

Abruptly freeing herself, Randy moved away. Travis' eyes narrowed. Could he—would he—kiss her like that to break down her resistance? Sick at the thought, totally bewildered and upset, Randy whirled for the door.

"You'd better talk to Aunt Corinth," she flung at him, escaping to the kitchen where she stirred the big kettle of split pea soup and began slicing bread and cheese. She heard Travis pass through but didn't look toward him. His footfalls stopped for a moment as if he were hesitating. Then he moved on.

She stopped holding her breath then and went about setting the table.

Neither man stayed for the simple meal. Aunt Corinth's apparently glum mood matched Randy's, and they didn't talk much. After dishes were done and the cage birds settled for the night, the women moved as if by unspoken agreement to the quilting frame and went to work with their needles.

In and out, over again. The stitching was slow but the inches grew, binding together front, filling, and back. In and out, in and out—stitches that would hold long after the makers were gone.

"It's as if the front is the future, the middle is now, and the back is the past," said Randy. "I wonder what's the thread that holds them together and the needle that drives?"

"I suppose the needle's purpose or aim, whatever a person works for." Aunt Corinth smiled, entering into the fantasy, evidently as pleased as Randy to find something peaceful to talk about. "And the thread is life itself; but the strongest strand in the thread must be love. Thread that doesn't have lots of that in it won't give; it shreds and breaks and is forever getting snarled and knotted." She gave Randy a shrewd glance. "You must be thinking an old maid's a funny one to go on about love."

Randy had, in fact, and flushed but her aunt only chuckled though her tone was a bit rueful. "There's been lots of love for me, Randy. First my parents and then your father, my littlest brother who was like a son. I've loved my birds and animals. Although I let them go, I can hear their wings in my heart and feel the warmth of their bodies."

She added defiantly, chin up, as if admitting a crime, "And

I've loved Micajah, too. Yes, I have. All these years. And though it seems odd, that loving never weakened or rotted my thread; it's been a strength and pride."

Randy put down her needle, utterly astounded. "Then why don't you tell him?" she demanded. "For heaven's sake, Aunt Corinth, you've got good years left, you could be happy together! It—it's downright wicked to act as if you didn't care!"

Aunt Corinth bent over her stitching. Her voice was so low Randy had to strain to hear. "Maybe—he doesn't care any more. He hadn't been around me, not really, for almost forty years. Maybe he's in love with what I was, not what I am."

"Fudge!" said Randy.

To her dismay, a tear dropped from her aunt's nose to the quilt, followed by another. And another.

"Don't!" Randy cried, springing up to look for a tissue. "He's probably discouraged. No wonder, the way you treat him! I'll bet if you let him see how you feel, you'd be needing this gorgeous quilt a good while before I do!"

"I won't marry a hunter!" Aunt Corinth gritted, scrubbing her eyes ferociously with the tissues Randy had brought. "If nothing can come of it, why start?"

"Maybe he'd stop hunting once you were married. Don't you think, Aunt Corinth, that he might possibly be stubborn, too? Too stubborn to give way till he's sure you really love him?"

Cider-colored eyes lifted hopefully, then dropped. "That's like marrying a drunkard in hopes of reforming him! Self-delusion, child. If I marry the old devil, he'll crow at finally winning and be off after his hounds lustier than ever." Giving herself a shake, she picked up her needle and resumed her role of elder. "Travis went off in a thundering temper and I don't think more than half was from thinking I'm senile or depraved to contemplate Brock Maynard's offer."

"He assumed I was behind that in some dark devious way," sniffed Randy, giving her needle a vengeful thrust. "I'm not going to bother arguing. He wants to think the worst. So let him!"

"No, child—"

Randy looked up, thrusting her chin out, realized it was her aunt's gesture and burst into laughter. Aunt Corinth joined in. At last, breathless, they stopped.

"So we're all stubborn," Aunt Corinth said. "Grandma used to say the polecat can't tell the buzzard that he stinks." Sobering, she added, "But you're young, Miranda. There's

109

time to strengthen the thread of your life with a lot of love. I hope you won't let pride or some mistake keep you from the man you ought to have."

"Even if Travis didn't insist on thinking me an exploiting huckster, he's courting Lettice. And I'm engaged to Greg."

"Are you?" asked Aunt Corinth equably. "Seemed a bit disengaged when you banged down the phone."

Randy's cheeks grew hot. "I did that so we wouldn't get into a really awful quarrel."

"Oh."

Sent into irritated silence by her aunt's bland voice, Randy stitched until Aunt Corinth yawned and said it was time they went to bed. But even though she was tired, Randy had trouble getting to sleep that night. She would turn from the horrid prospect of her aunt selling to Quality to her argument with Greg to Travis' searching, demanding mouth. There was comfort in none of these, only conflict, but at last she fell into exhausted slumber.

Valentino took fish from her hand next morning and seemed a bit more alert. Randy wondered in what way he missed his own kind, perhaps a mate and nestlings, and his home near the broad waters. Even if he got well, he'd have to start all over again, sort of an avian displaced person, and Randy felt sad about it as she went out to the porch to mix the woodpeckers' food.

Stopping to let Gronker taste the mixture and assure himself that it was in no wise as bill-smackin' good as his beloved mullets, Randy greeted Micajah, who was feeding the graceful herons and egrets, magical, mystical Arabian Nights birds, she always thought them, and put fresh food into the big cage.

The young woodpeckers and their purple martin cousin left off pecking and gossiping to wing or hop to breakfast. Woody cocked his head and bright eyes at Randy who laughed and made the kissing sound to him that had gotten him to open his mouth when he was tiny.

Crossing to play Penzance's head-waggling game for a moment, she noticed that the next cage was empty. Moses often left his pen for a few hours now but it was the first time he hadn't been there in the morning.

"I think he's struck out for good," said Micajah. "He may come back a few times out of habit or if he can't find food, but I think our little orphan who floated in on his nest is ready to seek his fortune. Fish, that is."

Randy felt a stab of loss, quickly superseded by gladness that the clever beautiful little green heron could go free again. "And I guess Penzance will be next," she said, knowing she would truly miss playing his gentle little waggling game and watching his green eyes light up.

"That's how it is," said Micajah. "A few have to stay but the whole idea is to let them go." His eyes brooded. Randy wondered if he believed some of her aunt's compassion and energy might well have gone to warm his life, and hers, too. Whatever he thought, all he said was. "It's a—*giving* thing, taking care of wild things you mean to set free."

He didn't stay for breakfast and Travis phoned to say he'd had an emergency but would try to get by that evening to look at Valentino. Randy did household chores, changed the spoonbill's papers, and oiled his feet. He had never shown the slighest impulse to peck her, but she still handled him with gloves and extreme care.

"I hope you didn't lose your family in that spill," she told him softly. "I can't imagine how you experience things, but a bird who can take over child-rearing to let his mate fly around a bit rates pretty high in my book. And how can people think you and other wildlings don't have feelings when just being in captivity can cause enough shock and stress to kill you?"

When you stopped to think about it, man knew very little about his fellow living creatures, especially those not domesticated. Scientists were still baffled by hibernation. Migration was a yearly wonder. The fine-set mechanisms governing mating, reproduction and habitat were dimly understood, if at all.

Wildlife, the Thicket, nature itself, were what Travis had called the secret, mighty, hidden heart of the world, pumping life to distant extremities that derided or forgot what they were ultimately grounded in. Until he could exist without air, water or food, man was part of a fabric. He should be careful how he cut it to his pattern, or one despised unraveled thread might totally ruin his creation, leave him as vulnerable and unprotected as his guns, oil spills, and bulldozers now left his sharers of the earth.

Settling Valentino in his box, Randy smiled, as always, at his comic expression, and washed up before going to see her aunt.

"Go for a walk," said Aunt Corinth abruptly. "You haven't

111

gotten out much, and you should. Just be sure not to get lost or leave the road."

"But—"

"Child, I need to be alone," said Aunt Corinth firmly. "Brock Maynard's coming for my answer tomorrow and I'm going to have it."

Randy fought back the urge to plead against selling. It was, after all, her aunt's decision, especially since she, Randy, wouldn't promise to see that the Redwine place was used by Redwines. So she kissed her aunt, said she'd be back for lunch and feeding Valentino, and set briskly forth.

The only time she had been out was last Saturday with Travis, so the region was strange once she left the clearing around her aunt's home. She would have loved to visit the orchid swamps and bird island again, but that would be a half-day hike even if she found the right way, so she followed the main road till a tire-worn track forked off from it.

Giant trees thatched the sky and banks of flowers and many-tendriled vines scented the air. Bees hummed, wings flashed, a squirrel streaked up a tree, scolding, and from a distance she heard a woodpecker's drumming, remembered a song of Micajah's.

"I," said the woodpecker, sittin' on a fence,
"Once I courted a handsome wench;
She got fickle and from me fled.
Ever since then my head's been red."

Had it been an ivory-billed woodpecker she'd seen that first day, never guessing it was almost extinct? She fancifully wondered if the Thicket had revealed a glimpse of its spirit, rebuking her connection with its despoilers.

Gentians, lilies, rose-flame azaleas, dogwood's shy white petals. The understory of maple, holly and hickory grew denser, crowding up to the wheel marks so that she began to glance back to be sure the woods hadn't closed solid behind her.

It seemed very quiet. Sun brightened the leaves above but no shaft reached the rich dark earth with its vines and ferns, mushrooms and toadstools, its changing array of blossoms.

And then she heard a horn.

16

Hounds burst from the dense underbrush, handsome creatures with sad, intelligent faces and long dangling ears, every shade of the dog rainbow but running to white with black and red-brown spots. Against the forest, they looked like something out of a tapestry. If there were just a unicorn . . .

The horn sounded again, close this time, from the opposite side of the road—trilling, mellow, silvery sweet. Summoned from their temporary pause at seeing her, the dogs loped forward as a man stepped out of the woods.

"Micajah!" Randy cried.

He was dressed in green and wore a battered brass horn hung from braided thongs looped across his shoulder. There was a sheath knife at his belt, but he carried no gun.

No gun at all. Yet he was out with his horn and his hounds. And he looked like a guilty little boy.

Randy stared. Blood mounted to the old hunter's white hair, and she was positive. She never had understood how he could be so careful and nurturing with the birds and then go out and shoot them.

"Micajah, you—you fraud!" she choked. "You don't hunt at all! You just run with your dogs and blow that horn!"

"What's the harm in that?" he demanded, scowling.

"Harm! Oh, Micajah!" Randy's laughter faded. "What a waste! All these years when you and my aunt could have been together!"

"I did hunt when we first fell out over it," he said as if defending his honor. "Been raised to it, never ran into anyone who didn't think hunting was natural till I fetched up against Corrie. But the Chances have always been hunters. I couldn't let a woman change me from that."

"What did change you?"

"Time."

"Really?"

"Maybe it was more what happened in that time. I hunted

for years but knowing what Corrie thought, knowing that she'd cry if she could see the foxes and coons and deer I bagged, took the fun out of it. The part I got to enjoy without any bad feelings was going through the woods with my hounds."

"When did you stop?"

"Ten, twelve years ago," he said reflectively. "My dogs cornered a fox and when it snarled at bay, its eyes were like Corrie's, its hair just the color of hers, and I tried to call off the hounds. It was too late."

Randy felt her head moving back and forth in disbelief. "And you didn't tell Aunt Corinth? You let her go on thinking—"

"I did go by one day. But she was nursing a coon that someone had hurt bad without finishing, and she just cut loose all over me, ripped me up and down and sideways. So I thought she hated my guts and there was no use talkin'." He sighed heavily. "I was wrong. Should have spoken out, no matter what she said."

"Well, you can tell her now, can't you?"

He shook his head. "No. I been studyin' over it while I've been helping out the past week or two. Corrie's got mighty set in her ways and I guess I have, too. Anyhow, I don't aim to let her boss me around. She can marry me like she thinks I am or not at all."

"Micajah!"

He gave his silver mane a restive toss. "Can't help it, honey. I'd tell her after she takes me, but if I hand her the buggy whip now, I'll never get it back."

"And you say the Redwines are stubborn!"

"They be, dang it." Micajah roughed back his hair. "If Corrie will have me, I'll do anything she wants because it pleasures me to pleasure her. But I won't be led by the nose or pecked at, either, and I sure won't put my neck under her foot as a starter!"

"Oh, Micajah!" Randy said again, between tears, laughter, and indignation, fearing that the two marvelous older people might go on robbing themselves out of sheer bull-headedness.

I can tell Aunt Corinth, she thought.

As if reading her mind, Micajah warned, "Don't you tell what you found out, girl, or I'll go marry one of those widows that's been offerin' to bake my biscuits! I love Corrie, always will, but my mind's made up on this."

She sensed that argument would only stiffen his spine.

"Mmm. Well, Aunt Corinth's trying to decide whether or not to sell to Quality. She sent me for a walk so she could mull over it alone."

"Corrie mustn't do it," he said. "She'd wither and die if she left that house. She's lived there all her life." He cast Randy a keen look. "Reckon she's disappointed that you don't plan on moving back. When she knew you were coming, I never saw anyone so happy and excited."

"Micajah!" said Randy grimly. "I won't be blackmailed, either."

Weighing her with frank hazel eyes, he gave a sudden nod. "Makes two of us, honey. But maybe I've been overdoing the absence treatment. Let's drop these dogs of mine off at my place and I'll come along with you before Corrie broods herself into doing something crazy."

Isn't it wonderful, thought Randy with a secret chuckle, how all we crazy, stubborn people try to protect each other from ourselves? Yet it really wasn't funny, or even thinkable, that her aunt and Micajah should continue to miss what both wanted simply because of pride.

They cut through the woods and at a real log cabin, Micajah ordered his hounds to stay. "Someday I'll bring you back to look around the place," he said. "My great-great-grandad built it and his son added on a couple of rooms. But right now, from what you say, I reckon we'd better get over to Corrie's."

A couple of the dogs sidled after them but Micajah ordered them back whereupon they sat down and howled mournfully. "Spoiled!" grumbled Micajah. "In more ways than one. When I stopped shooting, I gave my older dogs to my nephew and never trained the young ones, just kept 'em for company. They catch a rabbit when they can and corner coons and possums, but there's not a hunter in the lot and sometimes that makes me feel mighty guilty."

"At least you won't have to give them to your nephew if you and Aunt Corinth ever patch things up," consoled Randy.

"That's so."

Brightening, Micajah lengthened his stride. Randy had to exert herself to keep pace, so she was breathless when they reached the turn-off to her aunt's and saw a strange car in the drive. She was even more breathless when a man came to the door as they approached.

115

Greg!

He stepped out, ignoring Micajah, and took her in his arms. "Randy!" he murmured huskily. "My God, sweetheart, how I've missed you!"

His lips claimed hers. Her instinctive reaction was to draw back, keeping her mouth unyielding. It was like being seized by an intruder; it took her mind a number of seconds to instruct her body that she was engaged to this man, it was acceptable for him to embrace her.

But what her mind said, her feelings denied. She didn't, not at this moment, want Greg to kiss her. That seemed to get through to him, from the way she stood, motionless, and he stepped back cupping her chin, laughing.

"Still vexed? All right, darling, you may chide me to your heart's content, but could we lunch first? I'm starved. My flight managed to miss both breakfast and lunch, and all I got was three glasses of orange juice!"

"With vodka?"

His dark eyes laughed. "How well you know me!"

"But you don't know Micajah Chance," said Randy, and introduced them before leading the way in.

She left them chatting with Aunt Corinth while she fed Valentino and put together a salad and heated leftover onion soup. Micajah appeared to set the table, and slanted her a wink.

"Seems your young man and Corrie are hitting it off. He brought her a triple-decker box of Swiss chocolates and a cut-glass bottle of perfume." Micajah added in a glum tone, "I would have sworn Corrie didn't put any stock in that kind of frippery but she took on like a girl gettin' her first rose. Maybe," he conjectured darkly, "I should have brought her a pile of such stuff a long time ago."

So Greg thought he'd better get Aunt Corinth on his side. The judgment slipped through before Randy realized with some shame that she hadn't for a moment credited Greg with perhaps simply being nice. Maybe he was. She had no right to suspect what was, after all, a thoughtful gesture that had delighted her aunt.

Chastened, still baffled by her visceral rejection of his kiss, Randy adjured herself to behave though she felt it was high-handed of Greg to materialize without a word. Still, she hadn't answered his ring-back yesterday. He had some grounds for deciding he should clear up their problems at close range.

Only, bewildering and ridiculous as it was, Randy didn't want that range too close. Probably she was in a passing mood, but at the moment it was a physically, emotionally strong one and she did sense there were times when the head had to listen to the body and heart.

So she smiled at Greg when she announced lunch but sat at an angle which made it easier to look at her aunt or Micajah than at him. He seemed to guess her evasion, raising a quizzical eyebrow when their glances met.

"Miss Corinth was telling me you're quite a hunter, Mr. Chance," said Greg with genial interest. "Any bear left?"

"Still a few Louisiana bears," said Micajah. "Quite a few bobcats, a panther once in a while. The red wolf is about killed out but there's some coyotes and red and gray fox. Lots of whitetail deer, of course. And raccoons, otters, mink, beaver—"

He paused to think and Aunt Corinth picked up the naming. "Possum, ringtail, flying squirrel, gray squirrel, fox squirrel, skunks, armadillos, muskrats, cottontail rabbits, and swamp rabbits."

"Then there's the reptile critters," added Micajah. "Every poisonous snake found in North America and a bunch of lizards and plenty of alligators."

"Quite a Noah's Ark assortment," laughed Greg. "From what Randy said, I was afraid the big bad lumber companies had driven out our furred and feathered friends."

"They sure have where they've put in pine plantations," said Micajah. "Some birds, insects, and a few squirrels who can live on pine seeds may make it in those squared-off rows of slash pine, but there's no way for most creatures to survive." He shafted a chill hazel stare at Aunt Corinth. "How anybody who knows how it is can sell to lumber interests sure beats hell out of me."

"How anybody who pretends to care about wildlife can hunt and kill it is a mystery to me," snorted Aunt Corinth.

"Sweet mystery of life," murmured Greg, switching again to Micajah. "Is it true you use hounds and a horn, just like John Peel at the break of day?"

Micajah flickered a side look at Randy who clamped her jaws shut to keep from exposing him. If he insisted on maintaining his imposture and Aunt Corinth stuck to her principles, how would they ever get together?

Wretched waste, really stupid. But at least for now, Randy was afraid to interfere. Anyone mulish enough to conceal his giving up a bone of contention for a dozen years was entirely capable of, as Micajah had threatened, rushing into marriage with some mere bystander.

"The hounds are the best part of hunting," Micajah said, ladling up more soup. "Especially if they're cold-nosed hounds like mine."

"I thought all dogs had cold noses," said Greg.

Micajah chortled. "This is different. I mean my hounds can follow a cold trail, tracks that were made a good while ago."

"Really?" asked Greg in polite disbelief.

Micajah gave him a long level stare. "Sure," he drawled. "Once we picked up a trail and followed it half through the Thicket, through swamp and brush and bayou, and at last those hounds set up a whining around an old hickory tree. Nothing stirred, nothing, but the dogs kept on, so I reckoned something had to be there. Didn't want to climb the tree in case there was a panther or bobcat waitin', but the hounds stayed put and after a couple of hours, I just had to find out what was up there."

He buttered a hunk of bread and enjoyed his soup, till Greg demanded, "Well, what happened? What did you see?"

"I finally shinned up an oak tree right by the hickory," said Micajah. "Pretty soon I saw something white, inched over till I could tell what it was." He looked around the table and grinned. "Doggoned if the hounds hadn't picked up the trail of a possum that had been dead so long it was a bleached-out skeleton! So I knocked it down to them. They acted kind of sheepish and then hurried off to try to find another scent."

"If they hung people for lies, that one would have you on the gallows!" laughed a voice from the door.

Travis stood there. His gaze traveled to Greg, and his smile died.

17

Physically between the men, Randy felt skewered by their gazes, guiltily defensive toward both, so confused she couldn't speak. Fortunately, Aunt Corinth made introductions and invited Travis to join them.

"Thanks, no," he said. "Was over this direction and thought I'd look in on Valentino. May I?"

He lifted a sardonically questioning eyebrow at Randy, who colored and said, "Help yourself. He had a smelt about half an hour ago."

Travis nodded and went out. Greg's smile was rather tight. "Valentino?" he inquired.

"He's in Randy's bedroom," explained Aunt Corinth. As Greg's jaw dropped, Micajah smothered a grin and Aunt Corinth flustered on, "Valentino's a roseate spoonbill."

"A *what*?" Greg choked.

"It's a bird," Micajah gasped. "Got caught in an oil spill."

"My room's the quietest place," said Randy. "It's on the other side of the breezeway and no one's there much."

"Just visiting Samaritans?" asked Greg in velvet tones. "So that's the doctor who made clear to you the evil ways of Quality? You never said, Randy dear, but somehow I had him pictured as an ancient Piney Woods Albert Schweitzer of birds and beasties."

"I can't see that his age is important," flashed Randy.

"No? It does have a certain bearing on relationships, love." He made a courtly inclination of the head to Aunt Corinth. "Believe me, if this lovely and spirited lady were twenty years younger, you might find yourself jilted."

"Blarney, but I like it," said Randy's aunt.

"Well," said Randy, piqued and still rather upset, "Why don't you continue your mutual admiration in the living room?" She rose and began vigorously clearing the table.

"We'd best get out of her way before she throws us out

119

with the scraps," twinkled Aunt Corinth, reaching for her crutches.

Greg gallantly helped her up and they left the kitchen in a flow of joking laughter. Irritated by the whole situation, Randy flew into the dishes while Micajah dried.

"Well, if that just don't beat a hen a-lopin'!" he mused. "When I was young there'd have been a fight when two young bloods eyed each other like yours did!"

"Mine?" Randy sputtered. "Travis Lee isn't mine, that's certain."

"Is it now?" asked Micajah, all sweetness. "Then how come you squirmed when he saw Greg?"

Randy banged down a handful of silverware, took a long breath and said with dangerous calm, "Micajah, I adore you, but if there's anyone whose advice on romance I'd trust less than yours, it's Aunt Corinth. You two make up and then I'll be delighted to listen to you!"

He grimaced. "Fair enough, honey."

"If you'd just tell her the truth—"

He shook his head. "No. She takes me like I am or not at all."

"But she'd like what you are!" Randy argued. "It's what you're not that she thinks you are that's causing the trouble."

"I could say that I don't know what you mean, only I do," grinned Micajah. "Since Corrie's got plenty of company now, I think I'll catch a ride with Travis."

At the thought of being thrust into Greg's company alone, for after all, Aunt Corinth was pretty much confined to her chair, Randy panicked. "Oh, please!" she cried involuntarily. "Please stay around, Micajah! I—I—"

"Now isn't it strange that you aren't on fire to be with your fiancé who came all the way down here to see you?" poker-faced her friend. "Sooner or later, you've got to thresh things out. But I'll come by this evening to help feed."

"And stay for dinner?"

"If you want," he capitulated.

She gave him a quick kiss and he beamed. But after he had left with a stone-faced Travis, Randy sat down by her aunt and Greg with an impending sense of catastrophe.

Micajah was right. She'd have to confront Greg soon; but first she needed to confront herself. How did she feel about him, really? Was she temporarily upset because of their conflict over Quality or were deeper issues surfacing, attitudes that would inevitably undermine a marriage?

Greg and Aunt Corinth had been talking about some of the antique pieces in the room, and Randy's thoughts had drifted, but now she was recalled sharply to the present by Greg's patronizing chuckle.

"Amusing old fellow, that Micajah Chance. Perfect eccentric."

Aunt Corinth's eyes sparked and she sat up straight. "He's a fine neighbor and steadfast friend," she said, "whatever one thinks of his hunting."

"I don't know what to think of it," Greg laughed. "But if he hunts as well as he lies, he'd have to be terrific!"

"That wasn't a lie about the hounds!" defended Randy. "It—it was a work of art!"

"Wish all his hunts had ended like that," said Aunt Corinth. She sighed heavily. "But I guess it can't be helped. The Chances were always fools over hounds and hunting."

"Micajah's not." It slipped out. Randy, in confusion, bit her lip and hoped the remark would go unnoticed but Aunt Corinth sharply picked her up.

"What do you mean, he's not? Why, he runs summer and winter, fall and spring with those flop-eared dogs of his, even when there's nothing in season—" She broke off, eyes widening, sat absolutely still for a few seconds. "Miranda!" she said in a faint but imperious tone. "You know something I don't. What is it?"

"I—I can't tell."

"Why not?"

"I promised."

"But it's something I should know, isn't it?"

"Yes," admitted Randy unhappily. "But he said he'd do something perfectly horrible if I told."

Aunt Corinth went quiet again.

"Intriguing," Greg chuckled. "Who'd have expected all this drama? Any chance for a replay of the Hatfield-McCoy feud?"

" 'With his horn and his hounds in the morning,' " Aunt Corinth pondered. "I just wonder—" Her fox eyes lifted compellingly, pleadingly to Randy. "You don't have to say if I'm right, just tell me if I'm wrong. Micajah—he doesn't shoot. He's quit hunting!"

Relieved that her aunt knew while she hadn't, at least technically, violated the pledge Micajah had wrung from her, Randy decided it was no treason to add a little advice. "He's proud, Aunt Corinth. He won't stand for feeling black-mailed."

"Lord love him, neither will I!" Aunt Corinth gave what sounded appallingly close to a girlish giggle. "Relax, child! I've learned a thing or two this past forty years and now I can go ahead with a clear conscience, you'd better be prepared for a shock!"

Greg's bewildered look had grown to incredulity. "You mean all that hunter patter is a put-on, a big fake? Why, that old fraud!"

Randy's words exactly, but she didn't like Greg using them. "It's a long story," she said briefly. "And it's between Aunt Corinth and Micajah. Please don't let him know she's guessed his secret."

"Or that you tipped his hand?" Greg teased. "What sort of bribe are you offering, sweetheart?"

Randy refused to smile though she knew she was acting overserious. "I guess I don't like blackmail, either."

"Randy!"

Her gaze clashed with his surprised one. "It's clear that we need to talk," he said. "But I have to look up Brock Maynard. Why don't you come with me?"

"Please forgive me," said Aunt Corinth, "but I need to talk to Miranda, too, and as you can see, I can't whisk her away." She smiled beguilingly. "Could you spare her this afternoon, Gregory?" When he looked annoyed, she added, "I can't give Brock his answer till I've discussed it in detail with my niece."

"Oh." Greg's manner changed at once. "Sure, I can see where you'd want to talk over a step like that." He took Randy's hand, gave it a playful kiss. "But my turn's coming, angel! I won't be gone long but try to miss me a little."

Bidding Aunt Corinth a gallant farewell, he took himself off. As his car started, Randy's aunt gave her a thicker-than-thieves grin. "Saved you, didn't I? But now for long. You've got to make up your mind, dear. Who's to share your bridal quilt, Greg or Travis?"

"You're going to need it before I do," retorted Randy. "Anyhow, Aunt Corinth, Travis has plighted his troth or antiques or whatever to Lettice."

"They're not married yet. And neither are you."

Randy shrugged. "That's not what you wanted to talk to me about, is it? Or was that all a shameless hoax?"

"Miranda! Didn't I win you a little more time?"

122

"Yes, but—oh, I don't know what I think or want!" Randy gnawed her lip. "Why did Greg have to come charging off down here?"

"If that's how you feel, it's a good thing he did," said Aunt Corinth primly. "If you're not glad to see someone you're supposed to love, maybe it's because you don't love them."

"I'm just tired and—"

"Horsefeathers! Do you love him?"

"Of course I do! I—I think."

"Mmmph!" rumbled Aunt Corinth. "I don't hear any great assurance in your voice, my girl. I sure don't see it in your eyes! So you just be sure you don't do anything rash." She brooded for a moment, lifted her head abruptly. "Miranda, I'm not going to decide what to do with this place."

Staring, Randy wondered what her aunt was up to now. "I don't see how you can avoid telling Brock something tomorrow."

"I shall. I'll tell him to ask you."

"*Me?*"

"No other."

"But—but you can't do that!" Randy gasped. "It's your property. You have to make the decision."

Red curls bounced as Aunt Corinth shook her head. "No. You're my heir, the last Redwine. This house and land isn't my personal property. I just happened to be the one left living here. Ephesus and my brothers are dead." She nodded firmly. "Wouldn't be right to sell without your agreement. So you think about it."

"I don't have to think," said Randy. "I hope you won't sell, at least not to Quality."

"But what happens to the place when I'm gone?" demanded Aunt Corrie.

"I don't know," said Randy helplessly.

"Well, come up with some suggestions by tomorrow," advised her aunt. "This is really why I lured you down here, Miranda, to help determine what happens to the home place." She sighed heavily. "I didn't expect Quality to rush us along like this, but perhaps it's better to get it over with." She put her weathered hand on Randy's. "My dear, I know you have to lead your own life with your chosen man. I really don't expect you to drop everything and come here to live. But let's try to think of some way to protect the place after it passes from the Redwines." As if by telepathy, she picked up

Randy's thought. "Even if I marry Micajah, in ten or fifteen or twenty years, we'll not be here."

"I'll have a child by then who'll want to settle here," Randy suggested hopefully.

"Maybe. But till that happens, we need an alternative, something I can write into my will." Aunt Corinth peered at Randy. "I could, of course, just name you my heir and let you worry about the whole thing later."

Randy thought of what Greg would probably urge her to do with the place and knew that was one marital dispute they could do without. "No," she said hastily. "I'd rather it were decided now. As you say, it's really not a matter of personal property, it's a heritage."

She gave her aunt a quick kiss and went into the kitchen to start cheese and macaroni for supper, whipped up a pan of gingerbread to bake at the same time. It helped to have her hands busy as she wrestled with a dilemma.

What happens to a family place when the family's gone?

The only satisfactory answer was to install another family with the same values and of course Randy thought again of Travis. But he had his own old home. Besides, picturing Lettice and her brood in this house made the back of Randy's neck prickle with hostility.

But what was the alternative?

She could think of none. Her head ached and throbbed even worse to remember that Greg would soon be back. Too much was happening too fast. She couldn't stand pressure from him. But at least Micajah was coming, too.

And he was in for a surprise.

Randy cheered slightly at the prospect of the old lovers finally making peace; something that was far from her as she went about her evening chores.

18

Micajah turned up while Randy was feeding a much brighter-eyed Valentino. When she joined him on the breezeway, he was simmering with pent-up wrath and he stuffed vitamins into fish with such intensity that Randy shook off her own preoccupations to ask what was wrong.

"He's—he's given her the chaperone sofa!" growled the old man. "There she was with a couple of men and a truck, grinning like a Chessy cat! Dadburn her hide, now she's begun, won't take her long to move him over to her house, too!"

"Travis?" Randy's voice twisted raw and painful in her throat. "Lettice?"

"Who else?" asked Micajah bitterly. "And when I asked that flauntin' hussy what she was doing, she allowed as how 'dear' Travis had given it to her. Giggled and said they needed it over at Leffwell house though it wouldn't be long before they switched from a chaperone sofa to her great-grandmother's fancy fourposter." For the first time, he showed impatience with Gronker's brigand tactics, tossing his fish to the side so that the doughty cormorant had to scramble for it. "I've heard about her great-grandma—straight out of the New Orleans French Quarter, latched onto one of the feeble-minded Leffwells that turn up every generation or so. Travis Lee in that bed? Fair turns my stomach!"

It did worse than that to Randy. Even though she'd been braced for Lettice eventually getting Travis, Randy had vaguely hoped nothing definite would happen till she was gone when at least she wouldn't have to see it. She would have expected Travis to show at least that much decency. After all, he'd kissed her. And there *had* been something pass between them, there had!

Still, Lettice had warned her early on about their involvement. Randy had never consciously let herself spin dreams about Travis, but there must have been a lot of unconscious extravagance going on for her to feel like this. Chest tight, throat constricted with unshed tears, she hoped he wouldn't come by that night.

He didn't, but the evening was still far from comfortable. When the dishes were done and woodpeckers tucked away, Greg pulled a sexton's bench over near Aunt Corinth, drew Randy down beside him.

"Hither, wench," he chuckled. "I've barely seen you! And now the egrets, herons, cormorants, woodpeckers and roseate spoonbills are secured for the night, it's my turn for tender loving care."

Penelope chose that moment, however, to slip in through her doggie door, streak across the room, and flop on her back, waving her stubby webbed feet, giggling in adolescent abandonment.

"Penny!" Kneeling to tickle her, Randy laughed with delight. "Haven't seen you all day, you rascal! Bet you've found some playmates out in the swamps!"

"What is that?" demanded Greg, moving his elegant suedes as far as possible from the squirming Penelope.

"Penelope's an otter," Randy explained, and scooped the long sleek animal up in her arms, sitting down with her next to Greg.

"Won't she bite?" he asked.

"Won't you, when it seems appropriate?" countered Randy.

"Penelope may get carried away like a young dog," explained Aunt Corinth. "But she's not vicious."

Greg looked dubious, nor did he insist on closing the space between him and Randy as Penelope squirmed contentedly, gurgled, and settled into a drowse with her nose poked between Randy's ribs and arm.

"How's Brock doing with his land-buying?" Micajah asked.

"He'll get most of what he's offering for," Greg said. "Our rugged doctor friend won't part with ancestral acres, of course, but I went along with Brock to call on a Miss Leffwell and she's all but signed. She said as long as she's got some handsome old house in which to display her antiques, she doesn't care whether it's her family's or her husband's."

"I knew it!" gritted Micajah. "Knew it when I saw her bundling off the chaperone sofa! Don't know how the strumpet did it but she's finally nailed old Travis!"

"Is he the lucky man?" asked Greg. "Somehow I got the idea she and Brock—" Relaxing, looking highly pleased, he stroked Randy's hair. "Since the doctor's such a friend of yours, darling, we'll have to give them a suitable present. But no gift can be as splendid as that quilt your aunt is making for us."

"She should use it herself," Randy said. "I can wait on mine."

"Wait?" Greg laughed softly. "That's just what we shouldn't do any longer, sweetheart. Let's be married as soon as we can—right here in your aunt's living room."

"But—but—"

"Think about it," Greg said, touching her cheek. "I've already asked your aunt. She thinks it all fitting and proper."

Aunt Corinth said jokingly, "If you must marry a New Yorker, best you do it on the home hearth."

Randy felt besieged and assaulted. Marriage to Greg had always been in the future, a comfortable, unfrightening culmination of their personal and business association. Nothing to happen *now*, here in the old Redwine house with her aunt for a witness.

Nothing to happen when she might see Travis any day, Travis with his gray eyes that reached to her depths, Travis who had kissed her sweetly, devastatingly, though he had an understanding with Lettice.

"I can play for the wedding," Micajah offered, picking up the dulcimer.

"Why don't you play now?" suggested Greg, smiling good-humoredly at Randy. "Even though we've been planning to marry for a year, my lady looks a bit overwhelmed at my sudden inspiration."

Overwhelmed? Randy didn't know. If marriage with Greg was ultimately right, should an advanced date and altered location make her feel like this? She couldn't answer that. What she did know, deep in her bones, was that she didn't want to marry Greg *this* week in *this* room.

Did that mean she didn't want to marry him ever, anyplace?

At that point, certainty rooted in deep instinctive feelings deserted her. She refuged in closing her eyes to evade Greg's searching ones, listening to Micajah's pleasantly husky voice.

"I know where I'm going and I know who's
    going with me,
I know who I love but the Lord knows who
    I'll marry . . ."

And long after she had made the rollaway bed Micajah

and Greg set up on the breezeway, long after she had said her good-nights, Randy was haunted by the song Micajah was singing when she left the others, the old, old song, *Greensleeves*.

"Alas, my love, you do me wrong to cast me
   by discourteously,
When I have loved you so long, delighting
   in your company."

Mixed with the melody was Travis' expression when he had entered the kitchen that noon and seen Greg. He had looked—stricken. Yet how could that be, with voluptuous Lettice planning to switch from sofa to fourposter and her house to his?

Randy's sleep was fitful, dream-ridden, full of Lettice, Greg and Travis. When she heard an uproar, she thought it was part of a dream and drowsily shoved at her pillow, but the sound continued.

"Randy!" Was that Greg's voice? Tumbling up, she snatched on her robe and made for the door as the plea came again. "Rand—y!"

She stood blinking outside her door, stared as a seal-like body launched itself from Greg's chest, shot over to her, and collapsed in giggling, leg-waving glee.

"Penelope!" Randy choked.

A pungent smell assailed her nose. Greg came upright, tossing off sheet and coverlet—and a not-quite mummified fish.

"Ye—ech!" he shuddered, yanking a matching robe over red satin pajamas. "What the hell was that wretched beast up to? I felt something land on my chest and opened my eyes to find her eyeballing me with that loathsome fish in her mouth!"

"She likes you," Randy said, trying not to laugh. "She brought you a present."

Greg turned even paler. A peculiar look came over his face and he fled toward the bathroom he was sharing with Aunt Corinth.

"You *do* smell dreadful," Randy told the playful otter, letting her out the breezeway door. "Go take a bath in the swamp!" Fetching the rubber glove she used to feed Valentino, Randy held her breath as she gingerly picked up the fish and, following Penelope outside, tossed the malodorous object as far as she could past the banked honeysuckle and sweet-scented flowering thrift.

Rinsing the glove, she then hauled the coverlet out to the clothesline for airing and went to dress. Greg was nowhere to be seen as she went through the house to get Valentino's fish, but Micajah was there, fixing the morning feed. A faint reminiscent whiff swung her about to stare at him accusingly.

"Micajah! You—you did it!"

"What?" he asked blandly.

"Gave Penelope that stinking fish and let her into the breezeway!"

"Don't know what you're talking about," he said, but the corners of his mouth twitched. "Say, do New York men take morning walks in their p.j.s and robes? Saw Greg cruising around the front yard when I came in. Looked sort of puny. I hope the climate isn't getting to him."

"Climate!"

Micajah's hazel eyes went innocently wider. Randy groaned in frustration and hurried off to feed Valentino.

Greg, pallid but self-possessed, said little during breakfast but Aunt Corinth and Micajah kept up such a warmly affectionate exchange that Randy felt it couldn't be long till they pledged the love that had been between them for over forty years.

"Do you have our answer for Brock!" asked Aunt Corinth.

Randy scalded herself with a gulp of coffee. "I can't decide that, Aunt Corinth!"

"If you don't today, you'll have to soon or late," decreed her aunt. Greg and Micajah glanced back and forth between the two women as Randy frowned.

"What do you mean?" she asked.

Aunt Corinth shrugged. "Simply that if you don't have a reply for Quality, I shall tell Brock no and then make a will naming you as my heir."

"I won't marry her till she does that," grinned Micajah. "Chances never marry women for their money or land, just for beauty and spunk."

"Micajah!" Aunt Corinth turned rosy red. "Is that a proposal?"

"Corrie!" He reached across the table, cradled her hand in his muscular brown ones. "My whole dadburn life has been a proposal to you! You finally willin' to consider it?"

The phone pealed from the living room. Randy answered,

stiffened with surprise as Sue said hello over a rather poor connection and asked to speak with Greg. Micajah and Aunt Corrie seemed oblivious to everything but each other. Even so, Randy felt they should have some time alone and was glad when Greg joined her as she was clearing away the dishes and suggested a walk.

"Sue thinks I need to come back as soon as possible," he explained. "But I've barely seen you, darling! And we won't be missed around here for a while."

Pressure lifted from Randy in several ways, enabling her to agree almost enthusiastically to the walk. If Greg had to leave in a day or two, he couldn't expect her to marry him that quickly; and she still had three weeks vacation. That should give her time to sort out her feelings.

"Let me oil Valentino's feet and change his papers and water," she said.

He followed along, watching these procedures somewhat morosely. As she placed the spoonbill back in his box, Greg shook his head in bafflement. "You really don't mind doing that, do you? And you got rid of that putrid fish and hung out my bedding, and you stuff vitamins down fish you then feed to that host in the back yard. I'd never have guessed you could handle it."

"Some of it takes getting used to," Randy admitted. "The first night I was petrified that I'd drive a swabstick through a little bird's throat and I still think about something else when I'm stuffing fish. But it's such a good feeling when one of the birds can go back to its old life, and we've been lucky since I came. None of our patients has died. I really enjoy the work."

"And I suppose," angled Greg in a tone that was evidently meant to be teasing yet had an edge on it, "that like most nurses you've developed a case of doctor-adulation?"

"It's hardly the same." Randy felt herself color in spite of her cool voice. Rising, she went to wash her hands with rubber gloves still on, stripped them off and left them to dry over the shower rod. She washed her hands again, smoothed in lotion, and led the way out through the breezeway door.

The earlier smell of Penelope's overripe gift was gone. The breeze mixed with spicy and sweet and deep woods odors in a headily dizzying richness, the sun was bright but not oppressive. Randy drew in a deep tingling breath and turned to look back at the house guarded by the huge old magnolia, the banked lavender-pink thrift, delicate white bridal wreath, honeysuckle and jasmine draping the weathered clapboards.

"It's a charming old place," said Greg softly, taking her hand. "You love it, don't you?"

"Yes."

They walked on into the woods, their footfalls soft on the mulch of last winter's leaves and loamy earth. The inevitable woodpecker drummed faintly. A rabbit sped across the road. Wings flashed and the sense of life was everywhere.

"You could take the painless way out of your decision," Greg said at last. "Let her turn Quality down and leave the land to you."

"I can't do that unless I'm willing to undertake the eventual care of it," Randy said helplessly. "The only thing I'm sure of is that I won't opt for selling to Quality."

"So what does that leave?"

"I don't know," said Randy. "I just don't know."

Greg gave an exasperated laugh. "Sweet silly love!" he said, turning her toward him. His fingers brought up her face. She stood quietly beneath his kiss but nothing happened; the warmth and excitement and intimacy were gone. The mouth she remembered, involuntarily, was Travis'. The arms she longed to feel were his. Greg stepped back. His hands dropped with regretful finality.

"So that's how it is."

"Greg—"

He stared away for a few seconds before he managed a twisted grin. "It's happened, Randy. You're in love with the house or the Thicket or the handsome doctor. I'm not sure which, and I don't want to know. The operative fact is that whomever or whatever you love, it isn't me."

He was being decent, which made it worse. "No," he said quickly. "Don't say you're sorry. Good thing we found it out now—and a good thing you came to the Thicket while you can fit it into your life if that's what you decide to do."

By mutual silent consent, they turned and started back to the house. Randy's feelings were a mad confusion of relief, honest concern for Greg, regret and excitement. It was as if a stifling weight had been lifted and she was free to move.

But as they neared the house, her exhilaration died. She loved the Thicket but she couldn't live off her aunt. What could she do here to earn even subsistence? Perhaps she could get a job in Houston and visit the Thicket weekends . . .

And set herself up for running into Travis and his soon-to-be bride? Live on the fringes of both his life and the Thicket? No, at least for a healing, mind-and-heart settling time,

131

she'd have to go away. Greg spoke as if reading her quandary.

"You have your job, of course, if you want it, Randy. You do it well, and I can swear not to be a problem for you." He laughed. "You know, I never noticed it till she called this morning, but Sue has a darned sexy voice. Didn't you say I should take her to lunch while you were gone?"

"I did," nodded Randy. "When you take a fresh look at her, you're likely to notice lots of nice things you never saw before."

"Travel's a wonderful thing," said Greg. "And it's what I feel like doing! If I hurry I can catch an afternoon plane."

He was packed in half an hour, wished Aunt Corinth and Micajah much happiness, paused before he climbed into his car, took Randy in his arms, and gave her an almost defiant kiss.

"So long, darling." Pain turned his eyes even darker for a moment before he raised one shoulder in a shrug. "At least I won't wake up tomorrow with an otter and dead fish staring me in the eye!"

Randy broke into a delighted whoop at that and later she felt better about the way their romance ended when she remembered how they had both been laughing when he drove away.

Her mirth faded abruptly, though, as she went back inside. She had something to do. And then, if Micajah could take over her chores in a week or so, she had better follow Greg's example and get out of a place where the love she wanted was denied her.

"Are you still leaving this up to me?" she asked her aunt the moment she reentered the house.

"Sure am," said Aunt Corinth without quaver or quibble.

"Then let's call Brock, tell him no sale, and save him a trip out," proposed Randy. "As for what to do with the place—" She glanced from old fireplace to quilting frame, glimpsed the birds in the back yard, forced the words out with real pain because she was giving up claim to a world she had come to love, a world which she had no way of preserving and so must transfer to someone who would cherish it.

"I think Travis should be your heir. He'll carry on your work with birds and animals and he'll never let lumber or oil or whatever ruin the woods."

"But you love the place, child, and—well, since your

young man left so sudden—" Aunt Corinth floundered, amber eyes troubled, anxious.

"Greg was called back on business." She wouldn't say now that he had understood her better than she herself had, been generous enough to acknowledge the end of their engagement without reproaches or arguments. She could explain all that later. Right now she needed her strength and resolution to get through the moment gracefully and then stay till Micajah could take over. "I—I love the place, Aunt Corinth. Of course I do! But I can't take care of it the way that Travis would, I may never be able to live here." She knelt and took her aunt's hands. "It's the best way. Really."

"I somehow doubt that," said a voice from the door.

Randy whirled, scrambled to her feet as Travis lounged in. His gray eyes dwelled on her in a way that made her forget that he was Lettice's, that her blood mustn't race at the sight of him, she mustn't feel weak and melting just at the sound of his voice. He further undermined any lingering common sense she might have by coming over and taking her hands.

"I didn't hear all of what you were saying, or understand what I heard, but it sounds like a terrible bunch of moonshine even from a New York copywriter! Care to run through it again?"

She was hot and cold and her knees were boneless. Wordless, she stared up at him, heart seeming to wedge itself high in her throat.

"I left it to her to decide what to do with this house and land," explained Aunt Corinth. "She thinks I should leave it to you."

"That's crazy!" said Travis with tender ferocity.

"Sure is," said Micajah. " 'Specially when you're giving in to that Leffwell female! Never thought you'd do it, boy!"

Travis held on to Randy but he scowled at Micajah. "What are you rattling on about?"

"Saw it with my own eyes!" snorted Micajah. "There she was, latching onto that chaperone sofa and simpering over how you'd soon be using her bed instead!"

Travis emitted an unintelligible roar. When Randy belatedly tried to pull free, he hauled her against him in a grip that made her stop struggling.

"I'm not marrying her!" Travis thundered at Micajah. "She's gotten engaged to Brock Maynard, you conclusion-jumping old buzzard! I was so damn glad when she broke the good news that I gave her that sofa for a wedding present!"

He turned to Randy, gray eyes probing. "Did that piece of—of inspired hogwash have anything to do with that noble speech I walked in on?"

She nodded mutely, unable to take in the truth, mind faltering after his revelation. He wasn't Lettice's! He wasn't anybody else's! So—

"What about your New York guy?" Travis demanded.

"He's gone," chortled Micajah.

"Catching an afternoon plane," said Aunt Corinth.

Travis was still watching Randy. "Greg saw I—I'd changed," she stammered. "He—he was good about it, said I could keep my job—"

"Now what would you do with a job in New York when you're going to marry me?" asked Travis.

Randy's arms found their way around his neck and from a long way off she could hear Aunt Corinth chuckling.

"That's two bride quilts we're going to need around here this fall. Guess we'd better get to work on them."

Travis looked down at Randy and laughed. "If I get the bride, I can wait on a quilt," he said.

His lips found hers, and this time there was no need to fear or deny the kind of magic that grew with his kiss.

Have You Read These Big Bestsellers from SIGNET?

- [ ] **SANDITON** by Jane Austen and Another Lady. (#J6945—$1.95)
- [ ] **THE WORLD FROM ROUGH STONES** by Malcolm Macdonald. (#J6891—$1.95)
- [ ] **DRAGONS AT THE GATE** by Robert Duncan. (#J6984—$1.95)
- [ ] **PHOENIX ISLAND** by Charlotte Paul. (#J6827—$1.95)
- [ ] **CLANDARA** by Evelyn Anthony. (#W6893—$1.50)
- [ ] **ALLEGRA** by Clare Darcy. (#W6860—$1.50)
- [ ] **THE HUSBAND** by Catherine Cookson. (#W6990—$1.50)
- [ ] **THE LONG CORRIDOR** by Catherine Cookson. (#W6829—$1.50)
- [ ] **AGE OF CONSENT** by Ramona Stewart. (#W6987—$1.50)
- [ ] **THE FREEHOLDER** by Joe David Brown. (#W6952—$1.50)
- [ ] **LOVING LETTY** by Paul Darcy Boles. (#E6951—$1.75)
- [ ] **COMING TO LIFE** by Norma Klein. (#W6864—$1.50)
- [ ] **MIRIAM AT THIRTY-FOUR** by Alan Lelchuk. (#J6793—$1.95)
- [ ] **DECADES** by Ruth Harris. (#J6705—$1.95)
- [ ] **THE EBONY TOWER** by John Fowles. (#J6733—$1.95)

THE NEW AMERICAN LIBRARY, INC.,
P.O. Box 999, Bergenfield, New Jersey 07621

Please send me the SIGNET BOOKS I have checked above. I am enclosing $_____(check or money order—no currency or C.O.D.'s). Please include the list price plus 25¢ a copy to cover handling and mailing costs. (Prices and numbers are subject to change without notice.)

Name_____

Address_____

City_____State_____Zip Code_____

Allow at least 3 weeks for delivery

More SIGNET Bestsellers You'll Enjoy Reading

☐ A GARDEN OF SAND by Earl Thompson.
(#J6679—$1.95)

☐ TATTOO by Earl Thompson.   (#E6671—$2.25)

☐ FEAR OF FLYING by Erica Jong.   (#J6139—$1.95)

☐ MISSION TO MALASPIGA by Evelyn Anthony.
(#E6706—$1.75)

☐ THE BRACKENROYD INHERITANCE by Erica Lindley.
(#W6795—$1.50)

☐ MAGGIE ROWAN by Catherine Cookson.
(#W6745—$1.50)

☐ TREMOR VIOLET by David Lippincott.
(#E6947—$1.75)

☐ THE VOICE OF ARMAGEDDON by David Lippincott.
(#W6412—$1.50)

☐ YESTERDAY IS DEAD by Dallas Barnes.
(#W6898—$1.50)

☐ LOSERS, WEEPERS by Edwin Silbertang.
(#W6798—$1.50)

☐ THE PLASTIC MAN by David J. Gerrity.
(#Y6950—$1.25)

☐ THE BIRD IN LAST YEAR'S NEST by Shaun Herron.
(#E6710—$1.75)

☐ THE WHORE-MOTHER by Shaun Herron.
(#W5854—$1.50)

THE NEW AMERICAN LIBRARY, INC.,
P.O. Box 999, Bergenfield, New Jersey 07621

Please send me the SIGNET BOOKS I have checked above. I am
enclosing $_____(check or money order—no currency
or C.O.D.'s). Please include the list price plus 25¢ a copy to cover
handling and mailing costs. (Prices and numbers are subject to
change without notice.)

Name_____

Address_____

City_____State_____Zip Code_____
Allow at least 3 weeks for delivery